BUB
1°°

D0659040

Boy

A journey of love, friendship and
little white lies, discovered while in
the fight against the monster Dementia.

Anna Hamilton

Copyright 2018

All rights reserved by Anna Hamilton.
ISBN: 9781980214779

This book is a work of fiction. Names, characters, places and incidents are products of the authors imagination or are used fictitiously. Any resemblance to actual events or locales or persons, living or dead, is entirely coincidental.

Cover and book design: Anna and Sarah Hamilton

BOY is dedicated to my clan, the Hamilton's. Without them, there would be no me.s is our story:

Boy

My name is Boy. It is a name that was given to me by Old Man's wife. Old Man is the one who found me. Wife is the one who saved me.

This is our story:

I have no memory of before that day. The day I woke up on my back, lying in a pile of leaves in someone's yard, afraid and unable to move. I had no idea of where I was or how I got there, but I remember feeling relieved that I was lying on my back rather than my stomach. To be face down, with only a view of the dirt and all that crawls within it, would've been my doom for sure.

Sprawled out above me was a canopy of massive tree limbs. Slivers of an aqua sky peeked through the woven branches, shielding me from the direct sun, yet allowing me warmth and a view. I'd guessed that it must be October, possibly even November, because I could smell the rot and decay of a summer's growth. A cool breeze brought with it the scent of naked fields after a harvest, confirming the time of year. How I knew this I didn't know for sure, but the knowledge calmed me, enough so that I began to watch the squirrels run around through the brown leaves, scavenging acorns and anything else worthy of stashing for the up and coming winter. I watched the squirrels run up and down the trunk of the old tree, back and forth and up and down they went. I was relieved that they paid no attention to me.

Remnants of a rope poked through the bark of one of the limbs, exposing a long-abandoned swing, a remnant of another time. To my left was a house, a small white house with faded yellow shutters. Flower boxes hung below the windows, empty and rotting, falling away from themselves board by board onto the ground near where I lay.

To my right I could see the side of a barn along with roof tops of other small buildings tucked in alongside of it. I struggled to see more, but the pain in my head forced me to stop. Exhausted, I closed my eyes and oddly enough, I fell asleep. The slam of a door shook me awake and instantly was reminded of how vulnerable I was. I tried to turn my head towards the sound, but the pain limited my ability to move anything but my eyes.

I was petrified when I saw an old man and the shell of a woman come into view, walking in my direction, their footsteps growing louder as they shuffled through the dry leaves. I closed my eyes and held my breath, hoping I would be invisible to the shufflers slowly heading my way. I was terrified that the next crunch would be me. When the crunching stopped, so did the warmth of the sun. A chill ran up my spine when I realized that they hovered over me, blocking the rays of the morning's sun.

I opened my eyes just wide enough to take a peek and sure enough, there standing over me was the old man. He bent down a little closer to me and, when he did, the wrinkles on his face fell forward, exposing sad, investigating eyes.

I blinked once, maybe twice, and then he blinked once, maybe twice. Then he straightening his crooked body and said; "Wife, take a look at this little guy. This must be what hit our window this morning." At least now I had a clue as to why I lay in this yard, unable to move. I closed my eyes again, only tighter this time, hoping they would both just disappear. But when they didn't, I thought I might as well face my fate. If death was coming I sure didn't want to miss it. So, one more time I opened my eyes and simply watched them watch me.

The old man waited for no reply from the one he called "Wife", an itty-bitty thing with short gray hair and a blank stare dulling her hooded topaz eyes. She wore a flowered dress, stained from the meal of yesterday and possibly the days before that. She was close enough to me that I could smell urine. The stench was strong and fresh, not old like the food painting her dress.

Tightening his arm around her small frame, the old man tried to steer her away, back through the yard to the house with the faded shutters. She mumbled something and shook her head in refusal, moving just far enough away from him so that her feet were planted inches from where I lay. Another step and I would be flat as a pancake.

Tears filled the Old Mans eyes as he pleaded with her to return to the house for a hot cup of tea. But she ignored him, pointing down at me, then attempted to bend down, Old Man grabbed hold of her like his life depended on it, but I guessed it was more her life than his, maybe both, who knows.

I looked away from the dead eyes looking down at me. I looked to

2

the sky and then to the tree, frantically searching for the squirrels. I searched for anything to look at but Wife, because when I looked at her, Death is what I saw looking back.

Still pointing she whispered "Boy." Old Man cleared his throat. "What?" he asked. "What did you say?" He leaned in and put his face close to hers, hoping for more, and at that very same moment a gust of wind swooped in from across the fields, claiming the loose leaves from the ground and taking with it some of the thick emptiness that surrounded the two who stood there.

The power in the wind nearly knocked the old woman over, despite the strong arm still clutching her little waist. Like an anchor in a storm, he held on, and once the wind subsided, Old Man gently straightened their bodies. As he did, she turned and faced him "Boy", she repeated firmly.

Something sparkled behind her eyes. I saw it and I think Old Man saw it too, because a grin spread across his face as he finally succeeded in steering her around towards the house and away from me.

My heart was pounding so hard that I looked down at my chest, fully expecting it to explode right there and then. When it didn't I stole a glance in their direction. I watched the two crooked bodies shuffle through the leaves and into the little house.

Once they were gone, the autumn sun shined down on me again, warming my aching bones. I was safe for the moment, though physically exhausted from fear. At last, I fell asleep again

OLD MAN AND WIFE

Old Man sat his wife down in a worn but familiar wooden chair, one of the six that he made so long ago for his new bride and anticipated family. The chairs matched the carved oak table. Once glowing and clean, but now dusty and scattered with crumbs, stacks of papers taking up most of its surface.

It was at this table that for sixty-one years they had their meals. It was there that they enjoyed their family and their friends. They laughed and cried at this table. It was the morning meeting place for the farm hands as they discussed the chores ahead. It is where their son Charly did his homework and spit out his peas during supper when no one was looking.

Now it is simply a resting spot for Old Man and Wife. The friends are gone; most of them dead like their families. There is no longer chatter or laughter or Wife's yummy home cooked meals. The farm is no longer worked by the family, but now is leased out. They'd gotten rid of all of the animals when Wife fell ill. The only remaining critters were a cat and a dog named Gladys.

There would be no more morning meetings over coffee and home-made rolls. All of the farm hands were now either retired or had moved onto working farms. The only thing left beside the two of them were the empty chairs and sadness for what had been. Sadness was the only guest that lingered.

Old Man was tired. It showed on his face and in the slow way he moved his tall, frail body about the kitchen preparing tea. It was clear that what little energy he had was reserved for the woman he loved with all his heart, the woman he vowed to care for so many years ago in a small country church on the vast open prairie, the same church his parents had married in. That church still stands, but is no longer a church, nor is there a prairie surrounding it. There are no more country weddings, funerals or baptisms celebrated within its walls. No longer can you hear the singing that once seeped out from the cracks of the old white church.

Now it's an office building for the housing development that swallowed up the land. Hundreds of homes looking just like the other with no character or thought now consume what was once bountiful farmland and rolling prairies. Few families in the county had resisted the offers from developers. Old Man and Wife were among those few.

Many farmers were drunk on the idea of so much money. For them it meant no more back breaking work, no more depending on the weather for everything they had.

Honestly, no one blamed them for it. Farming is physically taxing and every new season is a gamble. No, no one blamed them. The ones who didn't sell didn't sell because they couldn't imagine the lump sum of cash or even leaving the lands that had been in their families for generations. What they couldn't imagine was not being able to stand on their porch every morning and every evening to take in the smell of the earth. A seasoned farmer could read the weather by the smell of the earth and his life and that of his family depended on it.

They couldn't imagine their lives void of a rooster's call reminding them to get the coffee brewing for the crew that was soon to show up before the sun. They couldn't imagine living so close to another's home that you couldn't pee outside or run around naked if you chose. Nor could they imagine anyone telling them what to do with their land, ever.

It's true that farming is a hard way to make a living, but it's an honest living, rewarding those who do it in freedom every single day of their life. Hugh and Betty Roberts simply could not imagine another way of

4

life. So, they stayed put.

Hugh and Betty, had always believed their son, Charly, would take over the family farm, build a house and raise a family of his own on the land. But soon after graduating from high school he went off to college to become a veterinarian. Although he was home each summer for a couple of months to help out, his schooling was his priority, and a seven year one at that.

It wasn't a complete surprise to his parents that he wanted to become a veterinarian. Ever since he was able to walk he played doctor with the animals around the farm. Taking the pigs' temperatures, Charly was not afraid to swipe his mother's meat thermometer from the kitchen drawer to maneuver it up a pig's butt. He'd even tackle calves to the ground when he was no taller than they were so he could wrap a towel around their heads, claiming that they had mumps and needed treatment. His imaginary skills went on through his childhood and would later evolve into a teaching job at Iowa State University, 115 miles north of the farm and hometown of Ottumwa, Iowa.

Hugh and Berry were proud that Charly was doing what he'd always dreamed of even as they knew that one day the farm would become too much work for just the two of them. Selling was out of the question, so they decided to lease out their fields to other farmers. Thousands of acres of corn and beans would now be the responsibility of someone else and collecting annual checks while retaining their lands would be easier than they ever thought it would be.

Life took on an easy pace. In the mornings, before the sun climbed the river banks, Old Man and Evert, his friend of over 50 years fished the arms of the river running through the rolling farm lands. They caught whatever they could, only to release them back into the murky waters while Wife spent her days on the farm with the animals and volunteer work at their church.

Wife loved animals as much as her son, Charly had. She spent most of her days outside, happily feeding and tending to the livestock. It was not uncommon to walk into the barn and hear a one-sided conversation between Wife and a cow. But once she started naming the hogs and the beef cows, the butchering came to an abrupt halt, as did any future sales. Even the eggs collected daily weren't for sale. Instead, she gave the eggs away to the local Food Shelf or to others who wanted or needed them.

Eventually Old Man accepted that the critters who lived there were a part of the family and no longer a means of making a living. Whatever made Wife happy was what made Old Man happy. But that happy time was short-lived.

THE DEMON DEMENTIA

Old Man sat the steaming cups of tea down on the table and lowered his six-foot frame to sit alongside his wife. He watched her stare into the wallpaper, lost and in another world, a world beyond the walls his great grandfather built.

She didn't speak or acknowledge his presence. She rarely did anymore. It was something he didn't think he would ever get used to and the brief joy of hearing her utter the word, "Boy", just minutes before had already left his heart.

The afternoon sun shone through the front window, warming the room to a cozy temperature, but also magnifying the food stains on her dress. He could smell the urine that seeped through her now full diaper.

He was ashamed of himself. All of her life, his wife had taken pride in the way she kept herself and her home. He used to call her his 'shiny penny,' but those days were long gone and he was tired. He was tired of the wrestling matches and the terror on her face as he changed her clothes or bathed her little body. Too often it was easier for him that she be dirty.

Old Man received frequent offers from the women at their church, the newer Lutheran church in town. The one that they no longer were able to attend. They called once or twice a week offering to clean the home, bath his wife or simply sit with her for a few hours, to give him the break he so desperately needed. He always refused, but not always out of pride.

He knew that everyone was a stranger to her, even himself, and he wouldn't risk scaring her any more than she already was. Even so, looking at the dirty state she was in now broke his heart, like so very many things broke his heart over the past ten years. So be it, Old Man thought. He decided he would drink his tea and muster up the courage to give her a bath. In his heart he knew that she loved him, no matter what, and for this moment that is all that mattered to Old Man.

Lifting the now lukewarm tea to her mouth, he moved the rim of the cup around her lips hoping to stimulate a past reflex, which it did. Her head turned away from the wallpaper and her bony hand reached up to hold the cup by herself. He kept his large hand near just in case.

She took an apprehensive drink from the cup then quickly pulled it away. There was a look on her face of pain, like she had just burned her lips. Knowing full well that the tea was far from hot, he played along. He apologized and took the cup out of her hand. When he sat the tea on the table, she did something odd. She bent her head way down near the cup and then turned her face upwards, so that she was directly under him. Her childlike action made him smile.

"You silly willy", he said to her, still smiling. "Would you like some more tea?"

"No", she answered clearly, then straightened herself back up in the chair. "I want Boy", she said.

Shocked, because other than that morning outside she hadn't spoken a word in many months, he could only stare at her. Knowing that at any second she would return to the wallpaper world, he didn't dare look away. Then, to his amazement, she stood up and pointed towards the window.

"I want Boy", she repeated.

He quickly stood and grabbed onto her waist to steady her. Excitedly, she pulled at his shirt sleeve, pulling and pleading silently for him to walk her to the window. He knew this moment would not last but was grateful for it just the same.

He shuffled her across the creaky green linoleum floor and, by the time they reached the ray of sun coming through the window, it had happened. She was gone again, blank and back into the world he could not enter.

It was over and, he was angry at himself for being disappointed. Ashamed to have expected more, hoped for more. He'd promised God a long time ago that he would accept what came his way and be grateful for what he still had. And he was grateful, but he was tired and empty as well.

Old Man sat her down in the nearest chair, a worn leather recliner that was easy to get her in and out of. He knew it was pointless, but he asked anyway. "Would you like some more tea?" There was no response, no recognition. He really hadn't expected any, but talking to her was a routine, one he would never quit.

He stood at the edge of the chair and watched the sun work its magic on Wife's face. She quickly closed her eyes and fell asleep. She was safe now. With a tinge of guilt, he thought,' lucky booger.' Then, in the quiet of his home he announced to no one that he was going to go run her a bath then left the room.

Hugh sat on the floor and watched the water fill their old bathtub, letting his mind wander back to all of the times he had bathed his little boy in this very tub. He remembered the giggling and the splashing and the occasional crying from soapy eyes.

He remembered how he would wrap his little boy up in a towel and carry him in to see his mamma so she could give him the smell test, cracking them all up as she smelled his neck, his arms and feet, tickling

7

him as she went along.

Those were happy times, and even though he did his best to stay out of the past he couldn't help himself. He hungered for those times and accepted that where the good memories rested so did the sad ones, the ones that now ate him alive.

ONE BOY LOST

It was nine years ago that Hugh bathed his son for the last time. Charly was thirty-one years old and weighed only eighty-nine pounds at the time. His hollow blue eyes never left his father's as he was washed.

Old Man wrapped his son in a familiar towel, like he used to, then carried his man boy to the couch, tucking blankets in gently round him.

His mama sat on one end of the couch and he on the other. She stroked Charley's face and hair into the night, while Old Man talked to God.

But cancer had won. Charly took his last breath at 1:35 am. Numb and silent, neither Old Man or Wife left the couch until the morning came through the window where his wife now slept. Only then did they reluctantly let go of the most important person in their world.

The grief that followed was blinding. It was because of the grief that Old Man didn't notice what was happening to Wife. Little by little, the invisible monster called dementia was swallowing her up.

Remembering, Old Man hung his large body over the bath water and cried like a baby. Trying his best to muffle the sobs that escaped his mouth, he grabbed a towel and buried his face in it until he felt something warm rub against him. Removing the towel from his face, he looked down to see their cat, Mrs. Nickels, staring up at him. She had found her way in through the open door. Big and black with green eyes that said 'hold me,' she crawled into his large lap and began to purr. Old Man dropped the towel and picked up Mrs. Nickels, who instantly nestled into his neck. Soaking up the sound of her heart beat, he whispered. "thank you."

Mrs. Nickels and the chickens were now all they had left of the animals. When it became evident that Wife was no longer feeding the animals, but only wandering aimlessly down the road when outside, her husband realized how serious the situation really was. But knowing how much the animals meant to her, he took over the feeding and watering, . taking her with him each time. But even that had become too difficult to keep up. He couldn't take his eyes off of her or she would just vanish into thin air, creating panic, a panic which sometimes required the help of others in finding her.

Sadly, Old Man gave the rest of the animals away, refusing any money offered to him. He gave the hogs to Evert Heins, his friend and a good old boy he'd known since grade school. Evert had a small farm to the east of the Roberts.

The beef cattle he gave to Fara Kremer and her brothers, Chod and Dude. They lived to the west of the Roberts farm. They were also friends from the beginning of time, it seemed. Ever since, Fara and Evert gave the Roberts more than enough butchered meat to sustain an army. Finally, Gladys, the Roberts little cocker spaniel, just disappeared one day.

ANOTHER BOY FOUND

With Mrs. Nickels hanging over his shoulder, Old Man turned off the water and walked into the living room, fully prepared to coax Wife to her waiting bath. It took him a minute to realize that the chair and room were empty. Mrs. Nickels scratched his arm when she jumped from his grasp and took off through the living room, running past the empty chair, past the table and out the open kitchen door, like she was on fire. Frantic, he called his wife's name as he followed the cat outside.

He ran to the closest building, the chicken coop. Nothing there but chickens. Then he ran to the barn. Empty and echoing her name as he called it. He ran to the stables and then to the stock yard. Nothing.

Where could she be, he thought as he stood in his driveway searching the length of the gravel road and seeing only a cloud of dust that the wind swept across the field and road. A red fox dug in he ditch near where he stood. "Betty!" He called over and over as he ran through the yard and around to the front of the house. Tripping on the fallen flower boxes, he grabbed at the corner of the siding to keep from going down.

Breathless, he leaned on the corner of the house and that's when he saw her, sitting under the large oak tree next to the bird they'd found that morning. Relieved, but worn thin, he questioned just how long he could physically keep this up.

There was no hurry now, as long as he could see her. She was safe, so he continued to lean against the house catching his breath and letting his old heart slow down a bit.

Wife sat cross-legged on a blanket of leaves. He was amazed at her flexibility, considering her age. He watched her lean over the dead bird as her mouth began to move, like she was talking to it. But then he realized the truth of what he saw.

She was talking to it!

Unable to believe what he was seeing and hearing he pushed himself away from the house and cautiously approached her from the side. What he discovered wasn't that she was talking to the damn bird. She was singing to it!

Old Man watched as she rocked her body from side to side in sync with the lullaby coming from her nearly motionless mouth. He looked down to the dead bird to find it looking back at him. Not dead, but clearly very much alive.

He was surprised the little bird had survived, recalling the loud thud it made when hitting the window, plus he knew how birds were one of Mrs. Nickel's favorite meals.

Wife stopped singing and looked up at her husband. Right then another strong breeze swept across the field and into the yard, rummaged through anything in its way, including her hair. It made her look a bit like a mad scientist in a floral dress.

The singing stopped then and Wife pointed at the bird, saying clearly, "Boy", he didn't know what the fascination was with the bird and frankly didn't care. His wife was trying to communicate with him, which was all he cared about.

Old Man looked around at the dark clouds, sensing the oncoming storm. He decided it might be a good idea if he brought them both into the house.

BOY

I thought I was having a bad dream, a kind of de javu when I woke to the sound of leaves being crushed under someone's or some thing's feet, but before I could take a look there she was again, the same shell of a woman that was here before. This time she sat down next to me, singing and gagging me with her scent. I wondered why she was there. More than that, I wondered how the sound of something so beautiful and so calming could come from something so terribly stinky.

Then the sweet sound stopped. All of a sudden, I was being lifted by a huge hand, attached to it was the tall strong one, the Old Man. With my body completely covered I couldn't see what was happening. I ached and pooped myself. But the deep voice I heard was tender, explaining to the shell woman that rain was on its way and that they needed to take me into the house where it was warm. A little voice, probably the 'shell's', repeated "warm."

THE RESCUER AND THE RESCUED

A curious Mrs. Nickels appeared at their feet as Old Man and Wife wound their way through the fallen leaves to the house, never missing step. The parade came through the kitchen and continued into the open dining room living room area, where Wife automatically sat down in a chair at the table. Still holding the bird in his one hand, Old Man walked the few feet back to the kitchen to grab a dish towel. When he turned back towards the table he saw his wife in the one chair looking at him and Mrs. Nickels in another doing the same. He grinned and thought maybe it was time they all had lunch.

By the time he crossed back the few feet to the table, Wife's left hand was stroking the attentive cat. Exactly what was happening he didn't know, and frankly he didn't care because at this moment his table had lunch guest and he was going to enjoy every second of it.

With his free hand, Old Man quickly made a nest out of a towel that wife had embroidered years ago. The sewed-on image of a cow and the name 'Daisy' were still visible but faded. With his other hand, he laid the bird down in the middle of the towel. Knowing full well that one of his table guests would be very happy to have the little guy for lunch, he bent over and picked up the shoe box that doubled as a file drawer. Turning it upside down, he emptied years' worth of bank statements onto the floor.

Before he could sit down and transfer the bird, Wife had already cupped the towel in her hands and carefully sat it into the box. Old Man stood looking at her in disbelief. He hadn't expected her to remain in his world for so long. Fact is he didn't expect anything anymore. He wished he had timed her attention span, her here and now, whatever that was. But right now, he didn't need his trusty Timex to know that this was the longest period in many months that a part of her remained there with him

The loud grumble of his stomach snapped him out of his thoughts, out of his state of disbelief. Hoping Wife could remain long enough for him warm the soup and make tuna sandwiches, he left the table for the kitchen while keeping a watchful eye on her and the attentive Mrs. Nickels.

The worst that could happen was that Wife would fade back into the wallpaper and Mrs. Nickels would eat their guest.

As he prepared their plates he remembered the waiting bath. It could continue to wait. Everything else could wait.

Without incident, Wife accepted the spoonfuls of warm bean soup and the bite-size sandwich held up to her mouth by Old Man. So far so

good, he thought. Mrs. Nickels sat upright in the adjacent chair following the action, moving her head back and forth from the box to the large
hand full of goodness that moved across the table, never making a move
for either. Old man wondered if the cat could sense the small miracle
unfolding before them. He also wondered if he was losing his mind by
imagining what the cat was thinking.

In between feeding Wife her bites of lunch, Old Man took bites of
his own, seriously considering his state of mind. It wasn't that long ago
that he had pleaded with God to end their lives, to end the hell on earth
they were in. But when he woke the next day, disappointed by their still
beating hearts, he considered killing his wife and then himself. He had
enough pills for the both of them. He knew how easy it was to turn on
the gas and leave it on. Yes, he knew ways.

The only thing that kept him from acting on his desperation was the
hope of seeing their son again, in heaven. He believed that if he ended
their lives by his own hand that heaven's doors would be closed to him.

Watching his wife now, he shuddered at the memory. Guilt rode heavy
on his aging shoulders.

BOY

*Okay, so there I was lying in a damn shoe box, carried away from my
view of the sky, carried away from the squirrels and the safety of the
large tree. I shouldn't have lollygagged in the sunshine. I should have
ignored my pain and tried to fly away when I had the chance, but it's too
late now.*

*Now I am a prisoner and I am afraid. I look into the faces that sur-
round me, especially the furry one with hungry eyes, and swear that if I
ever get back to into the open air I will escape.*

BOX

From a hiding spot Old Man took out a pair of scissors and began
making holes in the lid of the box. He was fairly certain the air holes
would be fruitless, but he didn't think Wife could handle watching Mrs.
Nickels eat her "Boy" alive. Honestly, he didn't think he could watch
that either. They'd had enough death. Nope, when the bird died, as he
was certain it would, it would do so under the lid of the shoe box. Then

he would toss it outside for his Mrs. Nickels to carry away.

Anticipating the tide to change, Old Man seized the moment by cleaning up the dirty dishes. He wiped the table, admiring the beautiful old wood as he wiped the vacant area of the table and thinking that someday soon he'd tackle the piles of paper that cluttered more than half of its surface, possibly even file them away. He winced at the dumping ground it had become.

When he was done cleaning up, Old Man put the lid on the box and said out loud that it was time the little fellow got some sleep.

Looking at his wife he added, "And time for you to take a bath", he held his breath and waited for resistance, but none came. She looked up at him, then pushed her chair from the table and, with wobbly legs, stood up waiting for his trusted hands to guide her.

Mrs. Nickels was no longer interested and jumped down from her chair for another seat on the couch.

As he started to walk Wife toward the bathroom she suddenly put on the brakes. Here it comes Old Man thought, anticipating the familiar and painful wrestling match. But there wasn't one. She simply turned her head back towards the table and pointed. Not waiting for more, he maneuvered her around and backtracked to the table and to the box. With his free hand he picked it up and continued walking Wife through the living room and onto the waiting bath. Closing the lid on the toilet, he sat the box down on it and then slowly undressed his wife.

In silence he hung his large frame over the tub again, but this time the sadness didn't haunt him. He gently bathed his wife's little body while she stared contently over at the box. All was good in the Roberts home for now. The only thing he wished for right then was that he had time to spare and to share it with someone.

By the time the bath was over they both smelled of soap and water, smelling almost as good as Old Man felt. Once he was done dressing her, he silently wondered where her mind was. Although she didn't wear the blank stare he was accustom to, she wouldn't look at him. Her attention was still on the box that now sat on their dresser.

Was there magic in that box? "Silly man", he said out loud. Old Man didn't want to press his luck, but at the same time thought that maybe, just maybe, it would be a good time to feed the chickens. He'd forgotten them in all of the morning excitement.

He wanted to take Wife with him. Lord knew they could both use some fresh air. If the rain held out they could walk the long driveway to the mail box and turn around and call it a day, and a good one at that.

These had become chores he did in a rush while Wife slept after breakfast. They were tasks that he no longer enjoyed, because he practically had to run as he did them, always eager to return to the house before she woke up, fearful of what could happen during those fifteen minutes he would be gone.

The driveway was a quarter mile long, and because of his fear and anxiety he no longer walked it. He drove his pickup or four-wheeler instead.

"How about we go outside?" he asked his quiet companion, helping her up from the side of the bed, adding a sweater to her shoulders, just in case.

Quick on the draw, her arm shot up and pointed towards the dresser. "Of course, we can't forget the bird", he said. "Boy!" she quickly corrected him. Smiling, he grabbed the box from the dresser and handed it to her.

"Okay, Boy", he said, and out into the late afternoon they went. Wife held tight onto the box. She was the keeper of it for now. She stood in the small space of the chicken coop watching his every move with an expression on her face that he couldn't place. It wasn't one he'd seen before or at least not one he'd seen in very long time.

He threw the meal down for the chickens, and since she made no effort to walk away he stole a few extra minutes to shovel out the old straw and replace it with new.

On both sides of the driveway there were fields of corn, now harvested. Even in the wind you could hear the pheasants running through the few dry stalks that remained. The distant fence lines stood like loyal soldiers waiting for the day they could come home. The air smelled wet and of dirt, the smell one becomes addicted to after having lived off the land.

As they walked the long driveway arm in arm, Old Man got a whiff of his childhood. All around him he smelled the seventy-eight years of his life. He turned to look at his wife who still clung to the small box and wondered whether she too could smell the years in the wind.

The rain looked like it was still miles away, however the wind was strong and present. In Iowa, the wind is never far away, always sneaking around, reminding you of how pointless it was to comb your hair or wear a cap.

By the time they had reached the mailbox it had started to sprinkle. Old Man let go of Wife's arm long enough to retrieve the mail and shove it inside of his flannel shirt, when a gust of wind swept by them, taking with it the lid from the box. Across one field and into the next it tumbled, until being captured by the loyal soldiers.

A shriek escaped Wife's mouth, her reaction unexpectedly quick.

14

Before Old Man knew what was happening she grabbed the bird from the box and stuck it inside of her dress, tucking it inside of her bra, right between the breast that smelled of soap and water. Then, with a devious grin, she lifted the box up and then let go of it. Out into the fields it went.

BOY

I was being bounced around in the dark for what seemed like forever when the bouncing suddenly stopped and dark skies appeared before me. I wasn't ready! I hadn't expected the chance of escape so soon.

Rain pelted my face making it impossible for me to see beyond it and before I could think of a plan Wife grabbed a hold me. I could hear the protest from Old Man as she put me inside of her dress, next to her body in some other nest. It was warm and I could breathe, but I feared I was trapped much worse than before.

They were almost to the house when Wife veered sharp to the right, pulling Old Man back towards the chicken coop. Rain was now more than a sprinkle, running down their faces, and matting their hair to their foreheads. As the rain ran down his weathered face and neck, Old Man remembered another time, a time before Charly, before marriage, before the years had carved their lives and before sadness knew who they were.

THEN

That morning after his chores were done a young Hugh Roberts biked the eight miles to Betty's house to help her finish her chores. The long ride down the gravel roads in the blistering heat was always worth it. Other than at school or church, it was the only time he could see her. It was the only time he was allowed to be alone with her. Rules for young adults were so different then.

They were in the chicken coop collecting eggs when the rain came. Betty held the basket of fresh eggs tight to her waist and, when the first thunder roared, she jumped, dropping the basket to the ground and breaking all of the gathered eggs.

With good intentions the two of them got down on their hands and knees to pick up the shells and slime that covered everything, including some of the chickens. Betty's long brown hair brushed against Hugh's shoulders. They laughed at the impossible feat of retrieving the eggs; that's when he kissed those perfect pink lips for the first time.

He was startled when she stood up and ran out into the rain and at first, he thought she was running away from him. But she wasn't. Instead, she danced and twirled around as the rain soaked them both to the bone. She was no longer afraid of the thunder and lightning or the scolding that was sure to come from her mother. That's when he knew that she was the one for him.

NOW

Wife pulled on his arm to follow her lead, bringing him back to the here and now, wherever that was. She pulled him into the chicken coop, where the rain made music on the tin roof.

He could tell by the vacant look on her face that she didn't know what to do once inside, so he sat two wooden crates on end, making seat for them both.

They sat on the crates facing the rows of nesting chickens, listening to the cooing and the pounding rain. What was left of the afternoon sky came through the two little windows on each side of the building. Soon it would be dark outside, but he didn't care. He was in no hurry.

He peeked at her from the corner of his eye, wishing he could steal one more kiss from those lips, but he didn't dare. He didn't want to frighten her. Even though she was the one who led them there he couldn't count on that it was because of anything she remembered.

When total darkness came, with regret for what was no more, he guided her back into the house to dry off and have some supper.

Old Man didn't dare ask about the bird in her bra. He couldn't be sure that she knew it was even there. He assumed that it was smothered by now. The thought of it wedged in between her breast and up against her skin disgusted him, but at the same time he knew that, dead or alive, taking it from her was going to be tricky.

The past year, Wife's memory had dissolved to complete dust, as did her ability to feed, dress or potty herself, and anything else for that matter. Her memory prior was poor at best, but she would have moments of clarity, which was what kept Old Man going. That and his love for her.

When they first learned that she had dementia a friend had given them the movie, "The Note Book", suggesting that it would be an opportune time for them to see it.

The movie was a beautiful but sad and a romantic portrayal of dementia. It was about a husband who altered his life for his sick wife, and for her wonderful moments of clarity. It was about the commitment two people make to each other and the journey that commitment took them on.

Old Man took that commitment very seriously, however, because of the sugar coating in that particular movie and a little denial, Old Man banked on the possibility of such times with his wife. He walked away from the movie with an unrealistic view of what was to come, which created even more anxiety and disappointment. Wife walked away from it angry and more afraid than she had ever been in her entire life.

Once she was officially diagnosed it seemed to all happened so fast, or at least that's what he told himself. He chose not to recognize that for years he had been covering up for what she wasn't capable of doing or knowing or remembering, and by the time he acknowledged that it was a disease and not grief or normal forgetfulness, she was in the thick of it, depending on him for almost everything.

The worst part were the unexpected bursts of anger and the combative way she fought him. He could live with all else, but the having to restrain his wife is what broke his heart.

After finishing up the rest of the bean soup and the peanut butter crackers he had added to their dinner menu, he cleared the table and returned from the kitchen with a wet cloth intending to clean Wife's face and hands. Old Man approached the table and stood next to her chair with the towel. Wife looked up and held out her hand, which he automatically put into his own.

She shook her head from side to side, freeing her hand from his, and again held it out. Curious, he dropped the towel in her hand and watched as she wiped off the table. When she was done she handed the towel back to him, stood up and walked by herself into the bedroom. Looking at the towel, he said, "Okay then, let's get ready for bed", and hurried behind to the bedroom.

Without incident he changed her into her nighties, removing the still little bird from her bra, then covered her up in her own little nest of quilts. He could feel her eyes on his back as he carried the bird towards the dresser. He could also feel the tiny heart beating against his hand.

"Tough little booger", he mumbled as he opened the top drawer. "I'll put him on my handkerchiefs so he'll be as comfy as you are, and in the morning, we will all have breakfast together. How's that sound?"

When no argument came, he laid the bird on his stack of folded hankies, turning it over so it was on its back. When he did this the bird's eyes opened.

He knew it was absurd to think that the bird was studying him, even listening to him, but that's how it seemed. Did the bird understand the word "breakfast?" Did it know that he might not see the morning light?

He closed the drawer, feeling kind of sorry for the damn thing. When he turned around, he was surprised to see Mrs. Nickels nestled in alongside of Wife, who still wore smudges of peanut butter on her face. Her left hand had found its way out from underneath the quilt to stroke the sneaky cat. Old Man knew the cat was no dummy. She smelled the peanut butter, an easy treat he was certain she would have as soon as he left the room.

Before turning off the lights, he glanced over at the drawer to be sure he closed it, satisfied the cat wouldn't be having the bird as well as peanut butter. He said "good night you guys", turned off the light and walked into the living room. Then he said out loud, "Lord, whatever it is that you gave us today, I sure would appreciate you bringing it back tomorrow." Then he sat down and fell fast asleep in his chair.

BOY

I could tell by the way he looked into my eyes that he's onto me. Old Man knows I am planning an escape! When the light comes back I will have a plan but first I will dream of what he called "breakfast."

That night Old Man dreamt of his boy, Charly. He dreamt of that awful day Charly came driving down the driveway, alone and unexpected, in the brown truck that read "Iowa State University" on its doors.

THEN

He'd made plans to meet Evert and his son Mike at the river later that day. They were going to the river banks in search of arrowheads, something they did often after the spring rains.

Arrowheads were one of the few things Old Man collected and he had accrued quite the collection.

Wife was in the back of the house making the bed and putting away the clean laundry that she'd just pulled off the clothes line. Old Man was standing at the kitchen sink cleaning up after breakfast when Charly came driving in.

He knew it wasn't Charly's day off. He knew his schedule and this wasn't one of those days. He remembered thinking that maybe Charly had been laid off or even worse fired from his job but he knew that would never happen. Maybe he needed something,.Something that couldn't wait until his next visit, something worth driving an hour and a half for. Curious he stayed at the window and watched his son get out of his truck and head straight to the barn.

After quite a bit of time had passed with still no sign of Charly he gave into his curiosity and walked outside and into the barn where the daylight and dust mixed together blinding him until his eyes could adjust to the natural light, the sound of sobbing stopping him from going any further.

Focusing through the dust he saw his grown son sitting in a stall on a pile of straw next to Bob, the Bull, Charly had raised from a baby. The bull had been born with defected rear legs making them much shorter than the front and worth nothing on the market. Old Man planned on putting the bull down shortly after discovering the defect, but Charly and his mother pleaded with him to spare the goofy looking critter, promising that they would care for him, which they happily did.

He stood frozen against an old post listening to his blonde hair blue-eyed man boy cry and talk to Bob. His body looked so small lying over his 450-pound friend.

"I'm sorry" Charly said to the bull "I'm so sorry" he blubbered. That's when Old Man pushed his lean body away from the post, and knelt quietly down on the straw next to Bob and across from his son.

"Hey buddy" Old Man said. "What's goin' on here?" With swollen eyes Charly sat up and looked across the bull to his father, snot and tears mixed together as they ran down onto Bob who with one large brown eye focused intently on Charly, his strong tail flipped up and down stirring up a cloud of dust around them.

"I'm dying dad, I'm dying, he blurted." Old man placed both of his hands-on top of Bobs belly to steady himself. "What do you mean son? I don't understand how could you be......dying?"

Charly wiped his nose on his sleeve, sighed and said "I've been having some trouble with my balance the past few months dad, my left leg doesn't want to move on its own", and looking into his father's eyes added, "I have to drag it behind me."

A moan escaped Old Mans mouth; Charly reached across Bob's huge rib cage and put his large hands on his father's large hands and said, "I was sure it was nothing, that's why I didn't call you and mom. But then my headaches started, so Eileen talked me into going to one of our colleagues at work just to ask some questions so I did."

Eileen was Charly's part time girlfriend, part time only because they were both committed to their jobs at the university. Their shift work made a personal life near impossible but somehow, they managed because the second part of the news Charly had brought home with him was that Eileen was pregnant.

Old Man held tightly to his sons' hands, afraid to let go, afraid to hear more. The barn was so quiet that when Bob farted it broke the horrible silence. Old Man and his son couldn't help but crack up.

They sat on the damp ground looking across at one another when their laughing morphed into a chorus of crying. Then they heard, "Old Man where in the hell are you?" They stood up and walked away from Bob hand in hand, ignoring the sound his strong tail made as it slapped the ground in protest.

They walked through the open doors and away from the place Charly had chosen to run, away from the safety and sanity he had known would be in there for him.

When Wife came into view all three of them stopped walking. She knew right away something was terribly wrong, she could tell by the way her men held onto each other and the raw agony on her baby's face. She fell to the ground at their feet and began praying to God.

Charly bent over and touched his mother's shoulder, interrupting her prayers by saying softly that he had something to tell her. "Mom, I have something I want to talk to you about" before she could respond he added "Don't you worry about God, I've already talked to him, now it's time I talk to you and dad. How about we go to the house so you can make us some coffee and warm up some of those sweet rolls I know you've got hiding in there?" which brought a half smile to her ashen face.

If you are women from the generations past you know that food represents more than just a meal, it represents love and togetherness, the energy spent coming straight from the heart. Your world and those in it revolve around the constant presence and preparation of a home cooked meal. It is a lesson these women learned without being told by their mothers and grandmothers. Feeding their people, gave them a purpose one cannot explain and more times than not that very food could cure most any woe, almost any.

Distracted by his request she stood up and wiped the dust from her dress. She looked from Old Man to Charly, searching for an explanation and when none came she replied "of course honey, let's get you to the

20

house so mamma can put some meat on your bones."

Old Man winced at the words she'd spoken, but regardless they followed the leader into the house, into the cozy kitchen that smelled of home.

Wife warmed the rolls and brewed a fresh pot of coffee, avoiding the eyes at the table. She chatted mindlessly about the new calf born a few days before and how it hadn't wanted to suckle from its mother but how today it's sucking like a pro. She went on and on about the calf until the coffee pot went silent. Then she went silent.

As if in a trance, she watched the steam rise from the cups as she filled them. For the first time in her life she was afraid to move, afraid to look at her two men sitting at the table. "Mom" Charly said, bringing her back to the task at hand. "I'm coming" she said, but before picking up the cups she reached over and grabbed the cross that for years hung above their kitchen sink and slid it into her dress pocket.

Once Wife sat down, Old Man reached for her hand under the table and squeezed it, telling her in his way that everything was going to be all right and to give Charly the floor.

Anticipating the news her son had driven all this way to tell them, she found herself staring, lost in his beauty. His curly blonde hair was long, way too long for a man his age she thought. His eyes like his fathers were so blue you could paint the sky with the color. He was simply beautiful.

Charly began talking and as he did he tied his hair up in a pony tail behind his head which made her chuckle inappropriately.

"I'm going to tell you guys the good news first okay?" Old Man looked down at his lap where his wife's hand had just returned the squeeze. Looking across at her, he knew in his heart that whatever was to be they would survive it as a team. That gave him the strength to look up and over at his son who then took center stage.

"Eileen and I planned on telling you this together but", he paused, but she couldn't be here today, so here it goes." Taking a sip of coffee, he continued. "We're getting married as soon as possible and we would really like it if we could get married here on the farm"

A squeal shot out of Wife's mouth, but before she could say anything Charly held out his hand as if to say wait, there's more, and there was. "I know you won't approve of the order of this, but Eileen is pregnant, three months pregnant." With that news, Wife removed her hand from Old Mans lap and put both hands over her mouth as if to prevent both the joy and judgment from spilling out.

"We didn't plan on it happening like this. We'd talked about getting married in the fall and then later start a family. We talked about Eileen taking a sabbatical once she became pregnant; between the two of us we make pretty good money and can easily live on one income. That was the plan anyway. Obviously now things have changed.

"I'm sorry mom, it wasn't supposed to happen this way." But with that, Wife got up and ran around to where her grown baby sat and hugged him.

"I don't care about order honey, what I care about is you and Eileen and having grand babies!" She released her hands from around his neck and raised them into the air, as if she was praising the lord which she probably was. "Old Man did you hear that? We are going to be Grand-parents" and then it came "Praise the lord and thank you Jesus!" With the widest of grins she bent over and kissed the Old Man right square on the lips.

"Mom, would you mind getting me a hot bun and some butter? I think I need some fuel for the next part", Charly said, giving his father a quick wink.

"Of course honey", Wife said and spun on her heels to fetch the hot buns from the kitchen.

Now, it was Old Mans turn to look into his sons blue eyes, they looked back at him with fear and sadness. Old Man said nothing as he reached over and squeezed his sons arm in support.

Charly stuffed his mouth with the homemade goodness, taking peri-odic sips of coffee, then shoving more sweat bread in as if prolonging the moment of truth. When he could eat no more, he faced his audience, who waited like Paul Harvey's listeners for 'the rest of the story'.

Clearing his throat, he said. "I came home today to tell you about Eileen and the baby, but I also wanted to ask you if I could move home. We would like to move home and as soon as possible.

Wife no longer had sense of any 'bad news', she left that sense out-side on the ground where it was now forgotten and replaced by the good news which she didn't think could get any better. When she started to get out of her chair to jump for joy or thank Jesus one more time, Old Man took a hold of her arm, it was a silent warning, telling her that Charly wasn't finished and to please stay seated.

Confused by Old Mans reprimand she blurted "of course you two - I mean you three" she said with a smile "can move home, nothing would make this old gal happier. When…?" again, Charly cut her off "Mom there's still more, please let me finish." Confused she nodded for her son to continue

"I have been having some health issues the past few months." Wife tried to interrupt again when Charly said, "Please mom, this isn't easy", she instantly knew what was coming was not going to be good, not good at all, she felt like she might throw up.

At this point you couldn't have torn her away from the table or the eyes that kept pleading with her to listen.

"A few months ago, my balance started to get goofy. I started losing the ability to stand for any length of time, without feeling like I was going to fall over-and I have a few times, fallen over. My left leg won't cooperate with the rest of my body, it's like my brain is sending signals that can't be received. I don't know if you noticed, but I'm dragging it behind me when I walk?" He didn't wait for a response.

"Then, I started to get terrible headaches. I was sure it was just a pinched nerve in my back so I went to a Chiropractor a few times, but when nothing changed, Eileen insisted that I talk to a doctor friend of ours at the University." Charly took a breath, then continued rapidly, as if he might stop talking if he paused even for a second.

"I told the doctor my symptoms and she immediately ordered a CAT scan, an MRI and a series of blood tests, which I completed last week.

Yesterday we were supposed to meet at her office, so she could go over the results with us, but I was too afraid, so I asked that she fax them to me instead, and she did this morning. After I read them, I just jumped in my truck and came home. I haven't even had the chance to talk to Eileen." With that, Charly took another deep breath. He was done.

Old Man looked over to his wife and watched the color drain from her face. As requested, she sat quiet in her chair listening to her son. Charly pulled the papers out from the inside of his jacket and laid them on the table in front of them.

"You can read them if you want, but the bottom line is…I have a brain tumor and it's sitting in the worst possible place that it could be. The doctor says it's inoperable, the prognosis is grim. I'll be lucky to live long enough to see my child born." Then he laid his head on the table and began to weep.

The second Charly put a period at the end of his last sentence, Wife threw up all over the table, the top of Charly's head and the papers she had no intentions of ever reading.

A month after 'the talk', Charly and Eileen had quit their jobs, emptied out their houses and moved what items they wanted to keep to the farm.

On July 8, 2006 with a few friends and Eileen's family at their side, they married in the old red barn on the Roberts farm. Pastor Dale from the Good Shepard Lutheran Church presided over them. If he judged the obvious lump Eileen carried in the front of the simple white dress she wore, he didn't let it be known.

It was a small, beautiful wedding. The day was to be all about the couple. Everyone that loved and cared for them made sure of that. Eliza Reeve, a friend of the Roberts from church had spent the entire morning out in the Iowa heat picking wheel barrows full of prairie flowers and grasses. The barn was refreshingly cool as she and a giddy Betty decorated the stall doors and makeshift pulpit. Along the floor and next to the folding chairs, they sat wooden barrels that over flowed with sweet grass and early wheat, blending appropriately with the lingering smell of manure and hay. Blue ribbons hung from the rafters and Hay loft. The Doves that perched in between the ribbons cooed as if they were hired to do so. It was perfect.

At Charly's request, Bob was present, so was Gladys and Daisy and running around at everyone's feet was a pregnant Mary Bell, Mrs. Nickel's mother. There wasn't enough room in the barn for all of the critters their son invited, so Old Man moved most of them out to the stockyard until the party was over.

The air was still thick with humidity as the sun went down on this day. Captured in its moisture was the aroma of growing fields, a roasted pig now devoured and the lingering embers from the bonfire that had blazed throughout the celebration.

Once the guest had gone, the bride and groom disappeared for the night leaving Old Man and Wife alone again.

After returning the critters to the barn, a pooped out Old Man retired into the house. Wife stayed outside in one of the empty chairs surrounding the smoldering fire, listening to the Oak crackle and spit out the end of its life.

When she stood up to leave, she looked around at all of the empty chairs, then out loud thanked the lord for such a perfect day.

She no longer pleaded with him to spare her child's life, she knew it was selfish and beyond his control, so instead she thanked him, for everything.

The same morning Charly died, his new wife was in the Ottumwa hospital having a baby, a baby boy she named Jacob. A crazy guilt was felt by all who welcomed this child into their lives. Torn between a new life and a new death Old Man and Wife couldn't or wouldn't leave their son whose wishes were to die at home.

Eileen didn't want to leave her dying husbands bedside, but was pried away from him by her parents when her labor pains grew too close and too strong. The sadness each of them felt for not being together was like an epidemic that lingered and consumed them and the many months that

24

followed.

Charly was buried in the family graveyard on the hill near the river, a short walking distance from the house. He was now with his people, generations of them. It was now their job to look after the beautiful blue-eyed boy named Charly.

After he died, the three of them busied themselves with the new little boy. They tried desperately to replace their grief with the joy a baby is supposed to bring to a family, but like empty vessels living under the same roof, they unknowingly poisoned each other by not dealing with their sadness and loss.

Old Man had hoped that this new boy Jacob, could save his wife from herself. Her absent mindedness a growing worry. Eileen, although attentive to her son was also void of any emotion, void of the obvious attachment that one has with their child. Concerned, Old Man called Eileen's parents and suggested they take her and the baby home with them for a while which they eagerly did. That was over eight years ago.

Eileen and Jacob remained at her parent's house in town. It turned out to be a good place to heal and get attached. Slowly, Eileen had morphed into the mother she had eagerly anticipated so many months before and her devotion to her son was unbreakable.

Once a week their daughter-in-law brought Jacob out to the farm, so Old Man and Wife could snuggle him and breathe in the air that escaped his little mouth. They were grateful to have Jacob and Eileen in their lives, but it was bittersweet watching him laugh and play and grow and change and then watch as they drove away from them.

NOW

Old Man woke up the next morning with a crimp in his neck from having slept in the chair all night. It was rare for him to sleep through the night; it was rare for him to have not gotten up at some point to go to the bedroom.

He stood up to stretch his old body and get his bearings straight, shaking the dream away he said something he always did in the mornings out of habit "Rise and shine everybody." Rubbing his stiff neck, he walked into the bedroom to wake his wife and found the bed was empty, the room was empty and the dresser drawer open. The bird was gone and so was Wife, again.

He called her name as he ran through the house, When it was clear she wasn't in the house, he ran outside calling for her. Before he could run to the back of the house to see if she was in the same place as the day before, Eileen's car came driving down the driveway.

She immediately got out of the car after seeing the panic on Old Mans face. "Hugh what's wrong? Where's Betty?"

"I don't know" he spits out, before taking off at a dead run around the house. Eileen followed him and behind her came a ten-year-old Jacob. They too ran around looking for Wife calling her name. "Betty? Grandma? Wife?" The chorus sounded throughout the yard.

Old Man ran from the yard to the barn, while Eileen ran down to the stockyard. Jacob went into the nearest building, which was the chicken coop, then ran back out hollering "she's in here Grandpa, she's in here."

The three of them squeezed their way into the small coop and found Wife busy gathering eggs in the front of her nightgown, scattered on the floor, under her feet were Old Mans hankies.

Eileen backed out of the building motioning for Jacob to follow and as she did asked "Hugh are you o k?" not taking his eyes off Wife, he nodded 'yes'. "Jacob and I will go make some breakfast, you holler, if you need anything." With a sad look on her face she shut the creaky door behind them.

He had known the day would come when he could no longer keep his wife safe. Standing there in the chicken coop, he feared that day had arrived.

"You scared me, woman" he said as he began transferring the eggs from clothing to a nearby basket. Not expecting an answer, he asked "what I am to do, sweetheart?"

Wife reached over with one hand and placed it on his arm, then with the other she pointed to nearby nesting box where he was surprised to see the forgotten bird, he looked down at his wife as she touched the birds little belly. She looked up into his eyes and answered "breakfast"

Just when he thought he could bear no more, her actions made him smile, giving him reason to doubt the constant feeling of defeat.

"Breakfast it will be."

He sat the basket of eggs on a shelf and went into her world, something her doctor suggested he do rather than the impossible feat of trying to bring her bring her back into his. He played along with her by reaching into a bucket of scratch; feed reserved for young chicks and held out a handful to her.

She turned away from his hand, but before the glimmer of hope he now felt vanished he watched as her crooked fingers reached into the dirty window seal and grab a clump of flies. In awe, he watched her hold

26

the squirming insects in front of the bird reminding him of all of the times she had saved a critter of one kind or another, like Charly had.

After a few minutes passed, he went for her arm to lead her out of the coop when the bird stood up and grabbed the flies out of her fingers with his beak, swallowing them up before falling backwards into the chicken box.

He couldn't believe it. She did it by God!

Tickled at her success, he waited to see what was next and what was next was a satisfied Wife turning towards the door waiting for his arm to guide her out, into the house where breakfast and a nervous Eileen and Jacob waited for them.

BOY

Wife stole me out of the darkness and took me to a different place, a place where other prisoners are kept. There are rows and rows of nests, humongous ones. She laid me down deep into one of them, grunted, then offered me food.

Once she left, I realized I couldn't see out of the nest. My only view was the occasional beady eyes that peeked over the box to check me out. Normally, that would have scared me, but I was still so hungry that all I could focus on was the smörgåsbord of food flying above my head making my dry mouth water in anticipation.

I laid there ignoring all of the curious eyes, instead I put my energy into trying to will the flying morsels towards me. I'm pretty certain my legs broken. When I jumped up to accept the "breakfast" Wife offered, a stinging pain ran from my leg and up into my head. I'm grateful it's only my leg and not my wings, a broken leg will heal which means I will be patient. When I am stronger, I am gone Johnson.

In the meantime, I will find out if the other prisoners know the way out of here.

NEW DREAMS FOR OLD

There were four sitting at the table, five if you include Mrs. Nickels, who sat in Jacobs lap begging him with her eyes to share a bit of his scrambled eggs and toast with her.

Eileen volunteered to feed Wife her breakfast, so Old Man could eat while it was still hot and without interruption. Her face gave away the concern and worry she felt for them. He loved her for that. He loved her for so many reasons and being at their table right then was one of them.

Old Man wanted to tell Eileen about the past twenty-four hours, but he didn't know how to explain that the recent events, which included terrible fear and helplessness, also brought some small miracles.

Wife's mouth opened easily to the spoonfuls of egg that came her way. Old Man thought it ironic that she accepted food like a baby bird might do, opening her mouth wide after each bite, silently asking for more.

Eileen and Old Man watched as she slowly ate her food, never taking her eyes off of Jacob. She was chewing far longer than necessary, long after the food was gone from her mouth.

Jacob teased the cat with his own meal, and when Mrs. Nickels stole the toast right out of his hand and took off running, Wife laughed out loud. Eileen looked over to Old Man and then to Jacob, and then all four of them were laughing.

When everyone had finished eating, Old Man led Wife to the familiar leather chair near the window and sat her down. Jacob was right behind him, offering an afghan to cover Grandma's legs.

"Sweet boy", Old Man said as he ran his large hands through the brown curly head at his side.

"Would you mind doing Grandpa a favor and feed the chickens? It's worth a buck to ya", he asked the boy. "How about two bucks?" Jacob shot back "How about no bucks?" Old Man answered, with a toothy grin "Okay Grandpa, a buck it is." And with that, he turned and skipped out the door.

Eileen and Old Man stood next to each other at the kitchen sink sharing in the dish duty. From there, they watched the late morning sun beckon for Wife's eyes to close, which they did, like clockwork.

Old Man wanted to talk to Eileen. He was hungry to talk, but he didn't know where to begin, so he just started babbling like a man who'd been in solitary confinement.

He told her about the fear of losing Wife - to the fields, to the road and of course to the nursing home. He talked about how the few chores he still had often went undone due to him not being able to leave Wife alone, which created the latest fear of not being able to keep up the farm. He cried when he told her about the fits of anger and how Wife fought him like a stranger when he tried to bathe or clothe her.

It seemed that many years' worth of sadness and fear poured out of him, but before he could get around to the good parts, the recent miracles, Eileen's heart could stand no more. She blurted out that she and

28

Jacob wanted to move back to the farm, something he had been waiting a long time to hear, and he told her so.

She told him about how she had talked to Wife several times about moving back and how she was waiting for them to give her the word, but that was before she realized that Wife was having memory issues. By then her own parents needed her.

Old Man shuddered as she told him about her parent's voluntary move into Silver Woods the week before. It was an assisted living facility in Ottumwa, one that Fara Kremer and her brothers financed from the ground up, which was no small feat.

Her parents told Eileen that they no longer wanted to have the responsibility of a home, something Old Man couldn't imagine. Her parents were excited by the idea of a community within a community, and eager for the many activities that were offered.

They were also relieved to free their daughter and grandson of care taking. Now someone else would be in charge of their medications and meals and doctor appointments.

"I begged them to stay at home, but this is what they wanted Hugh", Eileen said.

He grabbed hold of her like she had just handed him the cure to everything sick and evil and held her tight against his large chest. When he finally released her, he did so with an apology. "Honey, I'm sorry, but I can't ask you to give up the freedom your parents just gave back to you, only so you can return to the same isolation and responsibility. As much as we would love to have you here, I can't do that to you."

But Eileen wouldn't have it. "Hugh, this is what I want, it's what Jacob wants. This has always felt like our home.

I wouldn't be a prisoner here! I wasn't a prisoner in my own parent's home. That's not how I felt and that's how they felt. I wanted nothing more than for my parents to stay in their own home. I would have stayed with them until the very end and been okay with it, but believe it or not, they were bored at home. They said they felt like the walls were closing in on them. Living in town is not the same as living in the country, but you know that. Out here when you feel antsy there are options, like going outside."

She laughed but kept going. "Jacob needs the farm like you need the farm, but most of all Hugh, he needs a man in his life, someone to teach him the things I cannot. I'm lucky that Charly's life insurance made it so that I don't have to worry about money for a very long time, if ever. It has given me the freedom to be available to my son and my family in a way that I couldn't be if I was working. Please Hugh, let me share that with you and Betty."

Tears zigzagged down through the untended whiskers on Old Man's face as Eileen made her case. He knew that she and Jacob were the answer to his prayers, a gift from God, or possibly a gift from Charly. "Well, sugar, since you put it that way", he said, wiping his tears away."

Seeing his approval, Eileen raced ahead with her speech. "If it's okay, we could move in by the end of the week. I already have someone who wants to rent mom and dad's house and I could visit them in the mornings after I drop Jacob off at school, then he could ride home on the bus."

Clearly, Eileen had spent some time thinking about this move and the genuine excitement radiating off of her was contagious.

"It's a deal then", she said, sticking out her hand.

"It's a deal", he said shaking her hand in such an exaggerated way that made them both smile.

"I'll go tell Jacob the good news!" She said, heading outside. But first she turned around and said, "Thank you Hugh, thank you from the bottom of my heart."

Old Man watched from the window as Eileen headed for the chicken coop. "No, thank you", he whispered.

BOY MEETS BOY

Jacob was sitting on a shelf, squeezed in between the nesting boxes when his mom came into the coop. The coop was empty except for Jacob and Mrs. Nickels, who sat on the floor watching him.

"What's up bud?" Eileen asked, walking over to where her son sat."I thought you'd be outside feeding the chickens."

"I already fed them", he said. "Come here and look at this, mom."

Eileen walked closer to her son, following his eyes to one of the boxes. Inside the box was a little bird staring up at them, a sparrow of some kind she guessed.

"What the heck", she whispered.

"I tried to stand him up, but he keeps falling over", Jacob said, with concern. "I think he's broken, mom."

"Well then", Eileen said softly, "Let's leave him alone and let nature take its course, honey."

"But we can't just leave him out here to die", Jacob pleaded. "Can't I at least try to feed him?"

Eileen appeared to consider that. "You can try, but I wouldn't touch him any more than you have to. You don't want to give the little guy a heart attack before he has the chance to heal."

Eileen sat down on a wooden crate before acknowledging the fresh gob of chicken poop now stuck to her clothes. "Dang it", she mumbled. She watched her son successfully feed a bug to the bird. Taking his water bottle from his pocket, he dribbled water on his fingers and let the drops fall onto the bird's beak.

"You are your father's son, that's for sure", she said as she stood up and rubbed her butt along the rough wooden planks of the wall, removing some of the poop from the seat of her pants. "When you're done playing doctor, why don't you clean out the coop for Grandpa, I'm sure he would appreciate it."

And then before Jacob could protest she added, "As a matter of fact, this can be one of your daily chores from now on, now that we are going to be living here!"

With that news, Jacob started clapping his hands, but when he stood up to grab hold of his mom his jacket snagged the corner of the nesting box, turning it upside down and tumbling it to the ground.

It happened so fast that neither of them could catch the box before it landed, spilling its contents and the little bird inside onto the damp floor. Before they could pick up the injured bird, Mrs. Nickels snatched it up in her mouth and ran out the coop door and as if making a delivery, and dropped the bird in the middle of the pen. Quick and out of nowhere came one very large rooster who sat on the poor thing.

Horrified, Jacob screamed, "Shit!"

"What did you just say?" Eileen asked her son, of course having heard him loud and clear.

"I meant 'shoot,' mom, now what are we supposed to do?" He cried.

But Eileen decided that the time had come for expert intervention and said, "I have a feeling that Grandpa knows a little something about this bird, so why don't you go ask him to come on out here?"

Inside the house, sensing the commotion in the yard, Wife scooted her way out of the chair and, by the time Old Man reached her, she was standing.

"Boy", she said, pointing to the kitchen door.

Just then, Jacob came running in, panting. "Grandpa, you got to come help." Then he turned around and ran back outside.

Taking Wife's arm to steady her, Old Man said, "Well let's go see what's going on out there."

When Old Man and Wife arrived on the scene, Eileen and Jacob were surrounded by pecking chickens and one stubborn, immovable rooster.

"Grandpa", Jacob said breathlessly, pointing. "That old rooster is sitting on a little bird, and the hens won't let us get near it! It's going to get smothered if we don't do something quick!"

"Is that so?" Old Man asked. Then he stepped in closer to the gang of noisy chickens as Wife squeezed his arm so hard that it hurt.

"Boy", she said pointing to the rooster.

Misunderstanding, Old Man reached over and patted the top of Jacob's head. "Boy", he said to Wife.

But she shook her head angrily. "No", she said freeing herself from his grip. Then with little effort, Wife bent down and gently pushed the rooster aside, exposing the little bird with big black eyes.

She picked it up with cupped hands and, without a seconds hesitation, headed back into the coop.

Eileen searched Old Man's face for an explanation, but all he could do now was catch up with Wife

"I'll explain later", he said, adding, "If I can." Then the creaky coop door closed behind him.

Wife had already put the tiny bird back in a nesting box when Old Man came in behind her. He'd be damned if he could understand her fascination with this bird, but he had to admit that it was a pleasant distraction from the gloom filling most of their time together of late.

He decided then to go back into her world, to go with the only thing that seemed to be consistent in her mixed-up mind these days.

"Boy?" He asked, cautiously.

In a flash, she turned and faced him, wearing a smile and with a light in her eyes that said "Yes, you dummy!" Then she turned back around and gently patted the little bird on its head.

After a few minutes, she turned again, but this time it was because he was ready to leave. "House", she instructed as she held out her arm to her Old Man.

"Whatever you say, woman", he replied gallantly, and then for the second time that day, he guided her out of the coop and back into the house.

When they came through the door, Eileen and Jacob were back at the table waiting for them. Old Man held up his hand as if to say, "Later", then sat Wife in a chair across from them and sat himself down close to her. He looked across the table and grinned, he couldn't help it. He hadn't felt this good in very long time.

Then, turning his attention to his grandson, he said, "You know what I think, Jacob? I think it's time we get you an animal or two to look after. Maybe something you can take to the fair come next summer. How's that sound to you?"

Jacob stood up so fast that he knocked over his chair. "Really Grandpa, really? An animal of my own? Mom did you hear that?"

But, before Eileen could say anything Wife started clapping. Then they all joined in. When they realized that Wife had stopped clapping, their own clapping faded away into silence. The celebration ended almost as fast as it started, but it had been a great one, nonetheless.

BOY

This is going to sound weak, like I'm back peddling from my original plan. But for the record, I want to say that I'm no longer afraid for my life. I no longer fear that I am in the hands of the enemy, other than of course the furry one, who the jury's still out on.

It did grab me in its mouth. But it didn't hurt me, which it certainly could have. Instead it took me away to safety, to another prisoner who hid me underneath his own body, reminding me of my mother and how she kept me safe and warm the same way.

I miss my mother and wonder where she might be.

Don't get me wrong. I still plan on leaving when I am able, but now that I feel protected by those around me, I can be more patient. Food is available and so is the large nest that I wish I could see out of. The only other thing I wish for is someone to talk to, someone like me.

THE POWER OF LOVE AND MEMORY

After a late lunch, Eileen informed Old Man that she and Betty were going to clean out the bedrooms to get them ready for the big move-in on Friday, suggesting to the guys that they go outside and find something to do.

"Are you sure you don't want two big strapping men to help you move things around?" Old Man asked. Jacob laughed at that, but was eager to get outside. Relief was written all over his face when his mom refused the offer. "No, but thanks anyway. I think we can manage without you, can't we Betty?"

They all looked over to Wife who stood alone in the kitchen looking out the window. She didn't look at them or respond, not that anyone really expected her to. Talking to her and including her was done simply out of habit. It was something none of them would ever quit doing. She was a part of their world even if her world was filled with strangers.

Eileen scooted the guys out the door, then gently took Wife's arm and led her into Charly's old room and sat her down on the bed. Wife sat like a statue, watching every move Eileen made. Uninterested or unaware that she was surrounded in the leavings of her son's young life.

"This will be Jacob's room", Eileen announced, while removing the contents of the closet. She boxed everything away, purposely not looking at any one object as she worked. She would save those reflections for another day, a day when she could handle seeing the things that represented the man she no longer held or deal with the irony of his fading mothers memories, also boxed away.

By the time she finished with the closet and moved on to the dresser, Wife had fallen asleep. Still sitting upright on the bed, she looked like a rag doll, leaning to one side, ready to fall over any minute. Eileen eased her down and covered the little body in a blanket that once covered Charly. It no longer smelled of the man she knew. It smelled of must and dust and years of being ignored by a washing machine.

Next, she emptied the drawers of old clothes and various rocks that once had significance and put them in one of the many boxes at her feet. She saved out the arrowheads she ran across for Jacob's growing collection. At last she came upon a photo she couldn't ignore, much less pack away.

In it was a tall gangly boy standing next to a cow that wore a big blue ribbon around its neck. The inscription told her that it was taken in 1990 at the Wapello County Fair. A proud teenage boy stood with his hand on top one of his prized animals. As she studied the photo a voice behind her said, "Daisy."

Startled, she turned around to find Wife standing so closely behind her that it gave her goose bumps. She was looking at the photo as intently as was Eileen.

Once Eileen's heart went back to its normal rhythm, she led Wife back to the bed, where they both sat down.

"Daisy", Wife said again, not taking her eyes off of the photo. Pointing to Charly, Eileen asked, "Betty, who's that standing next to Daisy?"

A little laugh escaped Wife's mouth, "Boy", she answered. Not sure what just happened, but hoping it would continue, Eileen handed the photo to Wife and went back to the dresser and dug around until she found more photos of Charly. There were photos of him riding a horse, photos of him playing baseball and, in one of them he was standing next to a dozen other boys who all wore Boy Scout uniforms. She returned to the bed and displayed the photos in her hand like a fan.

34

"Who's this?" She asked, pointing to Charly in each photo.

"Boy, Boy, Boy", Wife said, tapping each photo with determination.

"Yes, Boy", Eileen repeated excitedly.

Eileen tried to prompt Wife into sharing more about the photos, but it was not to be. She couldn't. However, before fading completely away she reached over and took the photos out of Eileen's hand and forced them into the small pocket of her dress, crinkling and tearing them until succeeding. Then she lay back down on her son's bed and closed her eyes.

At first, Eileen thought that it was her way of shutting out the memories that flooded the now empty room. She thought that maybe closing her eyes shut out the pain inside of her soul, but when Wife began to snore, Eileen realized that the moment to reflect had simply come and gone.

There was no deep meaning or reasoning to any of it, which was disappointing no matter how many times it happened. Eileen knew dementia was unpredictable, like a train that runs on and off its tracks, out of control and with no one driving it. Even so, she couldn't wait to share this interlude with Old Man. She couldn't wait to help connect the dots that led from Charly to the bird Wife called "Boy."

By the time Old Man and Jacob returned to the house they were filthy and sweaty. They were talking about their great new plan as they came into the kitchen. As soon as Jacob saw his mother, he began rattling off all they had accomplished in the barn.

"Slow down kid, so I can understand you", Eileen said to her son.

It was apparent looking at Old Man how much he needed days like this one. His happiness was evident from the top of his head down to his dirty boots.

"We cleaned out the stalls to get them ready for my animals. I mean our animals", the boy gushed, smiling at his Grandpa. "First, we are going to get a cow, then maybe a pig or two, but first we are going to get a cow. And I'm going to name it Daisy, right Grandpa?"

When Eileen heard the name Daisy, she almost fell over. Seeing her reaction, Old Man went over to where she stood and took her hand. "Are you okay honey? You look like you just saw a ghost?"

"I think maybe I have", she whispered under her breath.

Concerned with the lack of color in his daughter-in-law's face he said, "Woman, I think you wore yourself clean out. How about you call it quits for the day while Jacob and I make some tea?" Not waiting for an answer, he added, "Where's Wife?"

Hanging onto the counter with one hand she answered, "She's in Char-

35

ly's room, sleeping."

It wasn't that he didn't trust Eileen, he trusted her with his life, but he also knew that Wife hadn't been in Charly's room for years. Neither of them had.

He immediately left her side and walked straight to Charly's bedroom where he stopped in the doorway as if he was afraid to enter. From there he saw Wife on the bed, asleep. Then he looked around, taking in the emptiness and the boxes scattered on the floor. After a few minutes he backed out and went to sit in a chair at the table.

Eileen hadn't thought about how he would feel about the changes she'd made in Charly's room "I'm sorry Hugh. I guess I wasn't thinking. I'm such a schmuck", she apologized.

Old Man held up his hand and said, "You're no schmuck, it's just a shock is all. You would think after all of this time we would be over it. To be honest with you honey, neither of us have stepped foot in there in years and that's certainly not your fault."

Eileen walked over and put her arms around Old Mans neck, hugging his head and shoulders. "We will get through this together, I promise you that, Hugh. Now how about Jacob and I make you a cup of tea. You look like you could use it more than I can."

He smiled up at her when Jacob piped in, "What in the hell is wrong with everybody? I haven't even got to finish telling you our plans."

"It's going to be awful hard for you to tell us with a bar of soap stuffed in your mouth young man!" Eileen said, walking back into the kitchen towards her terrified son.

"Whoops", Jacob said, running into the refrigerator as he backed away from his mother. "I'm sorry, it just slipped out", he looked beseechingly to his Grandpa to save him.

"Yes, it would be a good time for tea about now, don't you agree son?" Old Man asked Jacob as he tried to hold back the laugh that was beginning to escape from his mouth.

"I sure do Grandpa, and I'll even make it for you guys. Mom, go sit down and hug Grandpa some more while I make your tea."

That cracked up the Old Man. Eileen couldn't hide her amusement either.

"He just saved himself from talking with bubbles for the next couple of hours", she said before sitting down to join him in a good laugh at the table.

After tea and conversation about which animals they should get first, Eileen got up to warm the supper she brought with them. Old Man thought he'd died and gone to heaven as he ate the hamburger gravy,

36

mashed potatoes and home-canned peaches for dessert.

Wife was still sound asleep, which concerned Old Man. He checked on her a few times, making sure she hadn't slipped out the window or through a crack somehow. His fear of losing her was so great that even as she slept his nerves were on edge, which was obvious to Eileen. Soon she could help him full time. Soon, she thought, they would take shifts so he could take care of himself for a change.

She wanted to tell him about the photos and how Wife identified Charly in all of them. She wanted to tell him about Daisy the cow and the coincidence from earlier in the day, but Old Man looked tired and preoccupied. Heck, she was tired and preoccupied as well.

Deciding it could all wait for another day, they said their goodbyes. Jacob fell fast asleep as they drove away from the farm. The fresh air tuckered him out, which she believed was the best medicine... for anyone.

Eileen watched the sun disappear from the sky as she made the last corner to her house. Pulling up in front of it, she parked but didn't get out. She studied the house as her son slept in the back seat. She looked at the small yard and remembered the many games of tag played in it. She looked at the porch with its glowing overhead light and saw the familiar shadows reflected in the windows, which were always mysterious, scaring her as a child. The play house that was once the neighborhood hangout was partially visible from the street, standing as it did next to the cottonwood tree that was her refuge when she needed to disappear.

She knew that she could walk away from all of it and not feel guilty or sad. She knew because her parents walked away from it. They left to begin a new life for themselves while the choice was still theirs and she was excited to do the same for herself and her son.

Her parents, Bob and Kathy, were excited for something new. That's what her dad said as he finished loading up their van on moving day. Her mom was so giddy that she sat in the passenger seat long before her husband had finished packing the van. When her dad slid the door shut for the last time her mother hung out the window and said to Eileen, "Don't be sad honey, it's just a house. Our memories aren't inside those walls. Our memories are inside of us." Then she handed their house keys over to Eileen.

"We'll see you guys soon, once we get settled in honey." And with that, they drove away, like they were going on some exotic vacation. Those words had given her the permission she needed to do the same, to move on.

She looked up to the Big Dipper as she got out of the car and said, "Thanks mom and dad." Then she roused her son awake.

THE IMPORTANCE OF PURPOSE

The next day was much like the ones before except that Old Man woke with a purpose, one that fueled him. Soon the chairs around the table would be filled on a regular basis. Chatter and the smell of good food would fill the old and quiet rooms. These were little things that he had missed terribly, but hadn't realized just how much until right then.

He was excited at the thought of returning to the projects and chores he once enjoyed, thanks to Eileen. Just thinking about cleaning out the garden for next springs planting made his mouth water for fresh peas and tomatoes.

Soon he would have time to spend with his grandson, uninterrupted time. He would teach him about the farm and everything involved in making it work. But most importantly, he knew that his old house would feel like a home again and that realization filled him with joy and anticipation.

With breakfast over and Wife asleep in the chair, he decided that it was time to tackle the clutter he had ignored for so long on the table. He would make room for the ones who would soon be occupying it. By the time he finished sorting through the piles of paper, he was surprised that most of it was just junk, leaving little to even file away. Something that took years to accumulate took only minutes to throw away. "Imagine that" he mumbled.

He stood and looked at the empty table. Now it was too empty, so he went to the buffet standing against the wall in between the living room and kitchen and searched through the drawers until he found the most colorful doily he could find and placed it in the middle of the table, giving the table some life. But it still wasn't enough. So, he walked to the kitchen and grabbed the salt and pepper shakers, adding them to the doily. He stood back admiring his work. Then Wife woke up, with a whimper.

Standing her up from the chair, he found that she was soaking wet. No wonder she woke up, he thought to himself. "Poor baby, let's get you cleaned up and then we'll go feed the chickens."

She didn't look at him, but stared at something faraway. Today that didn't grab at his heart the way it usually did. He was slowly accepting that she lived in some other place, and he knew that he was lucky she was here at all.

In the bedroom, he apprehensively removed her clothes, and with a warm washcloth washed her legs and private area. As he did this, she began to hum. Relieved that she was no longer whimpering, and thrilled that she wasn't fighting him, he tried in vain to place the familiar tune while he worked.

After buttoning up the clean dress, she now had on, he took the wet clothes and tossed them into the nearby laundry basket. Before turning back around, something in the basket caught his eye. He reached down to remove whatever it was from the pocket in the dress she wore the day before, but it was so jammed in there that he had to lift the dress out of the basket and use both hands to pull it out.

When he'd succeeded, the blood rushed into his face, making him feel light headed. He sat down on the bed next to Wife and stared at the face that looked back at him.

He studied each torn photo with care, remembering the day each and every one was taken. For the first time, he realized how much his grandson looked like his Charly. It was also the first time he could look at his son and not be consumed with grief.

At that realization he asked, "How about we go see how your feathered friend is today? I bet he's one hungry Boy." The magic word had been spoken. She turned away from the other world and cocked her head toward him. Seeing the photos in his hand, she slowly took them from his loose grasp. She pointed to their son and said, "Boy."

"Oh my God", Old Man muttered, connecting the dots. "Let's go feed that Boy, woman!"

Old Man was filled with an energy that was powerful. The familiar despair that walked along side of him for so many months was nowhere to be found and he sure wasn't going to go looking for it. It would find him soon enough. Of that he was certain.

THE BIRD WHISPERER

Clouds filled the sky as they made their way to the chicken coop. Leaves danced in their path and circled the mob of hungry chickens. Soon the snow would come and cover everything in a blanket of white. He knew that if he was going to get Jacob some critters, he'd better get on it.

After supper he would call Fara and see if they couldn't do a trade for a young cow or two. He knew she could use the hay in his lower field and, with weather permitting, there was still time for her brothers to mow and harvest it.

He smiled when he realized that with animals on their way he could use some hay this winter himself. He hoped he could barter for some of the hay Fara had stockpiled. Just thinking about the hay filled his nostrils with the familiar scent.

Once they cleared the doorway, he released her arm so she could walk alone to her nesting Boy. Old Man left her alone in the coop while he fed the chickens in the open pen. There was no fear of her escaping without going passed him first. The worst thing that he figured could happen was that she would forget why she was in there.

When he was finished, he joined her inside, pleased when he walked in to find that she hadn't forgotten what was in there. She was sitting on the lower shelf, squeezed in between two boxes and holding the bird in the palm of her hand. She was humming the same tune that she had before, but just when he had the name of the tune on the tip of his tongue, the bird startled him by flying onto one of the window sills.

Wife started to stand, and Old Man instinctively held out his arm to stop her. He pushed an empty box out of his way with his other hand so he could sit down next to her on the shelf. They sat scrunched together like sardines in a can, watching the bird pluck imprisoned flies from the window sill and making Wife giggle in delight.

She turned to him, and at that moment he thought back to the many high school football games they went to, both at their school and then Charly's, sitting on cold bleachers, scrunched together like they were now, happily keeping each other warm.

Breaking his trance was her breath on his neck when she said the same words as before, but with pride. "Boy." It was the same pride she had when Charly scored a touchdown or ran the ball with those stocky legs of his down the field, dodging his opponents so many years ago.

He watched her turn back towards the window and the bird. He was so happy, yet so afraid at the same time. Even in the depths of her dementia she had insisted on saving this little bird from death, and she had succeeded.

He was in awe that a bird, a simple little bird, could stir up the tangled and dying memory of her life, of their life, when nothing else had. Not medication, family, friends or even her husband of a many decades. There was no way to explain it, not to anyone.

Selfishly, he worried that now that the mystery of the bird was over, so might be the joy it had brought into their lives. Surely, now that it could fly away, it would do just that.

After fifteen minutes or so had passed, Old Man stood up to leave, silently telling himself that what will be will be.

He held out his hand as support for Wife to step down safely, and when she did the bird flew out of the window sill and landed on her shoulder! Old Man stared in disbelief, Wife only giggled more as the three of them walked out into the cloud-covered morning. The bird teetered on her bony shoulder, clinging with its little feet to her dress. The chickens ignored them as they passed.

Old Man didn't walk the short distance to the house but, as a test, he walked them towards the barn, just to see how long it would take before the bird released its grip and flew away. It didn't take long.

As soon as they cleared the barn doors, the bird released the hold it had on the thin cotton dress and flew to a nearby rafter. When their eyes adjusted to the natural light inside of the barn, Old Man pointed to the bird, who perched on one of the large timbers, looking down at them.

Out of nowhere, Mrs. Nickels appeared at their feet, taking in the action too, until a mouse ran across the dirt floor in front of them. Then, as fast as her legs would take her, she was off.

Old Man knew this was it. For the first time since her disease took everything familiar away from her, he found himself praying that she would forget the bird, just so she wouldn't be let down by its departure.

As a distraction, he guided her over to the newly clean stalls, explaining unnecessarily and to fill a void, that soon Jacob's calves would be living there.

"Daisy?" She asked, leaning on the wooden boards that separated the stalls.

"No. I mean yes! Daisy will be here and so will Bob and Lord knows who else", he said with a chuckle.

"Boy?" She asked with searching eyes.

"I don't know, Wife. Maybe. Boy has to go home sometime. His mama must be missing him something terrible, don't you think?" He replied, reaching for anything to satisfy her obsession.

She put her hands on her chest and said, "Mama." That single word broke his heart, but he wasn't going to let it break his spirit.

"Yes, you are a mama, and a very good one at that", he added, covering her tiny hands with his own large ones. He would do and say anything that calmed her, even if it meant lying or, Lord knows, finding her another bird to focus on.

The little bird was the apparent substitute for the son she no longer had. At least that's the conclusion the dots had led him to.

They had almost reached the house when the wind arrived, blowing dust and leaves around at mach speed, touching each and every leaf that still clung defiantly to their branches, and creating a sound he'd loved since childhood.

Old Man shielded his eyes with his right hand and hurried Wife towards the kitchen door, when he noticed the chickens heading for the opening in the coop as fast as they could, seeking shelter from the wind. "Smart", he said into the face of the wind.

Before he took the last few steps towards the door, he saw something move out of the corner of his eye. At first, he thought it was a shingle on the chicken coop flapping around in the wind, but then he saw that it was a bird, a bird that looked very much like the one they'd just left in the barn. It stood on the edge of the roof to the coop, fighting the wind and watching the chickens scramble in through the hole in the building.

"Impossible", he thought. "It's just a sparrow. There have to be millions of birds in this state that look just like this one. But then, why was it there? Out in the weather when all of the other birds had sought shelter? This was either a coincidence, or he was losing his mind.

"How can this be?" He said to the side of Wife's head. "You're the bird whisperer, what do you think?"

Her head was turned down, avoiding the wind when he spoke to her. He didn't expect an answer, nor did he get one. It was partly out of habit that he asked.

Curiosity had gotten the best of him. He had to go check out this bird, and he had to take Wife along with him. There would be no more leaving her out of his sight, at least not until Eileen was there.

So, he turned her around and pointed "Would you look at that, woman? Your Boy wants back in his house!"

She had been mesmerized by a button on her dress when Old Man said the magic word. Her head jerked up to the sky, searching...searching.

"Over there", Old Man said, pointing to the roof and the strange little bird that stood on its edge, defying the strong wind. She immediately pulled away from him and headed towards the bird, when the darn thing swooped down and met her halfway, landing on her shoulder, again!

The hair on his arms stood up as he caught up to her, taking her arm as they neared the coop. As soon as he opened the door, the bird left her shoulder, flew in and landed on the side of the same box it had inhabited the previous two days. But a chicken had already beaten him to the nest.

Wife didn't appear phased at all by what had just happened. Nor did she want to linger. She simply reached over and pulled the string on the light bulb mounted on the wall, meant to radiate warmth on cold days. Then, when she turned to go, she whispered, "Nighty, night."

THE GIFT OF HUMOR

By the time they cleared the doorway, it had started to rain. It was a cold rain that sent shivers up Old Man's spine, matching the sensation of the goosebumps that still covered his arms.

Inside the warm house, Old Man made a pot of tea. But, before he took the cups to the table he reached inside the overhead cupboard and grabbed the bottle of brandy he kept for times of need, dumping a couple of shots in with his tea. He figured this was definitely a "time of need."

The Brandy burned as it slid down into his belly. It felt good, too good. Knowing he shouldn't have anymore, he got up and made them a couple of grilled cheese sandwiches instead, which were also pretty darn good.

In between bites, Wife fiddled again with the buttons on her dress. Old Man followed her eyes to the far end of the table where the old photos of Charly sat.

She released her hold on the buttons and reached over, sliding the photos in front of Old Man. He looked down at them, then back to her. She smiled, and that's when he decided that he was no longer going to be afraid of whatever ride they were on. Instead, he was going to ride it hard, right up until the end of time.

Outside, the wind blew so strong that the old shutters banged ruthlessly against the side of the house. After dinner, Old Man sat Wife in the leather chair near the window, and once she was settled in, they watched a variety of small items fly by the window, reminding him of the tornado in the 'Wizard of Oz.'

It had been years since a tornado touched down in their county, and many years more since the farm was hit by one. The memory added to the chills he felt, so he walked over to the thermostat and turned the heat on for the first time that fall. By the time he was back in living room, she was asleep. Full tummies do that to a person, he thought.

He knew he couldn't afford to fall asleep yet. The risk wasn't worth it, so instead he busied himself with the sign he was making for Jacob. It was a sign for the barn that read 'Jacobs Farm' in big black letters. He would hang it up next to the faded one with 'Charly's Farm' painted on. Maybe one day, Jacob would make his own sign, one with his own child's name on it, and add it to the barn. The thought was as warm as the brandy.

He had just finished the last bit of paint on the sign when the phone began to ring, startling him. He hurried into the kitchen to grab a paper towel to wipe the paint off his hands, but before he could get to the phone, the ringing had stopped, and he heard Wife say, "Hello?"

With all of the strange happenings lately he shouldn't have been surprised that she'd answered the phone. Anything was possible, he thought as he walked back into the room and burst into laughter when he saw that she hadn't picked up the phone at all, but a statue of Roy Rogers that sat next to her on the end table. She was holding it up against her ear, as if waiting for someone to answer her greeting.

He couldn't help himself. "Who is it?" He asked.

Sitting Roy back down on the table, she said, "They hung up."

"They'll call back", he said, laughing. And they did call back, but by then Wife was no longer interested. She had faded away again.

It was Eileen calling to check in and to let him know that Saturday was the big day. She told him how she and Jacob spent the evening packing up their things, and how she was taking a break before packing up the remainder of her parent's stuff.

She sounded pumped up and tired all at the same time. Before the call ended, he walked into the other room and quietly shared with Eileen what had just happened.

He was relieved when she cracked up laughing, relieved that she didn't judge him for finding humor in Wife's confusion.

To have a little humor, and to have it without feeling guilt, was a blessing he thought as he returned the phone back to the table, next to Roy.

That night, as he laid down next to Wife, he thought of the big day ahead. Only two more days before Jacob and Eileen would be moved in.

He kicked himself for not remembering to tell Eileen that Fara would be delivering the calves that day too. He was so excited that he didn't think he would ever fall asleep, but he did.

BOY

I was sure I would be stuck in that big old building for the night. Thank goodness for the cracks in the loft. They give me options for escaping that scary place. I wouldn't have slept a wink with all the noises and bats flying around my head.

It's much warmer in here and much safer too. Now that I know I'm not a prisoner, and that the ones who share these nests with me aren't being held against their will, I can relax a little and get some much-needed sleep.

My leg still hurts. I feel a burning each time I take off. I think I just need a little more time.

To be honest, I'm not looking forward to finding a place to hole up for the winter. With any luck, Old Man and Wife won't make me leave until I am ready. I would say that by spring my leg should be good as new.

Now if I can just get the fatso in my nest to move over a little…Come on, big mama, scoot over. There, now that's perfect.

What was it Wife said before she left? 'Nighty, night?'

FRIENDSHIP

By the time Saturday rolled around, Old Man was ready for big changes, ready for Eileen and Jacob to call this home, ready for the smell and sounds of animals to surround him, ready for some new life and all of the commotion it brings with it.

Old Man was just plain ready.

Fara told him that her spring calves were a gift, and so was the hay her brothers would deliver with the animals. "They'll be no arguing with me, Hugh. We're also going to cut your fields so you don't have to worry about 'em going to waste. Maybe next year, you can teach that boy of yours how to run a tractor", she insisted. Just the thought of that excited him to no end.

"How can I thank you, Fara?" He said, as he watched Wife sip her tea at the table.

"Hugh, I'm just so happy that Eileen and Jacob are moving to the farm. I'm relieved to know you won't be alone this winter with Betty. It's way too big of a job for one person. So please, there's no need to thank me buddy."

"Well thank you anyway. I mean it", he said with raw emotion in his voice before hanging up.

They had been friends as well as neighbors since they were children. They had both experienced a lot of good times and a lot of bad times in their lifetime. That's always the story, if you're lucky enough to live to old age. It's also one of the things that bind people together. Struggles and surviving them is what fills the pages of our history books. It's also what makes a friend a true one.

By the time breakfast was over, he could hardly contain himself. The anticipation was driving him nuts. Deciding to put the dishes off until later, he put on his worn out Carhart jacket, and by the time he approached Wife with a sweater she was lost in the wallpaper world, humming that same tune.

He sat down next to her and began putting her arms in the sleeves of the sweater, when she started to scream. When he tried to hold her the screaming grew louder, scaring the daylights out of him. "No, no, no!" She screamed towards the wall.

He scooted a few inches away to give her some room and to give himself some as well, then very softly said, "Shhhhhh, it's okay, baby. Shhhhhh, it's okay", he said this over and over until her screaming eased into a whimper. Turning to face him, she said, "I want my mommy!"

This was new.

"Well love, she's not here right now", was all he could come up with that quickly. It slowed the whimpering and ended her fascination with the wallpaper.

Cocking her head to one side, she asked, "Where's my mommy?"

"I guess she's in town running errands, but she'll be back later", he improvised. "She said that we're supposed to do some chores around here before she gets back."

Silence. But then a little, "Okay", escaped her lips, and she began putting on her sweater all by herself.

Old Man felt a sudden wave of nausea. Between the excitement of what the day was to bring, and Wife's new confusion, he knew he needed to get a grip or risk ruining everything. He needed to preoccupy himself with something.

The chores. He'd do the chores.

They were walking through the kitchen towards the door, when he remembered the mysterious bird and how it had appeared to want to be in the coop with the chickens. Impulsively, he grabbed the drill out of the closet. Maybe he could make a few improvements to the coop for the little guy, and drill a few holes for coming and going. Maybe even put up a perch or two.

Once they cleared the few steps and were safely on the ground, he glanced over at Wife. He was relieved to see the calm on her face. Whatever it was that had made her scream bloody murder was forgotten, at least for the present.

The only good thing about the disease that ate away at her brain was that it was like a slide show that presents a fleeting image, before quickly changing to another. Even if there were times he wanted the slide show to slow down, he was grateful that a few minutes before it hadn't, for her sake.

For the first time, he wondered what stage she was in. He knew there were different stages to dementia, but he'd never looked them up, or asked the doctor about them. It was like he had been living in a fog ever since she got sick. Dealing, but not dealing with what came his way, without any knowledge of what it meant or what was to come.

As the sun warmed his face one thing he thought was very clear; he could no longer predict what world she was living in at any given time. Her asking the whereabouts of her mother, who had been dead for decades, made him feel sad. Sad for the woman who shuffled along beside him, and really sad for the little girl inside of her who missed her mommy.

As they made their way to the coop, he thought of his own parents and how long they'd been gone from his life. It's funny how no matter how old a person gets, they never quit missing their parents.

All of it made him think about the God he was raised to believe in, and he wondered why such a powerful being would allow such torture of the good and the innocent. None of it made any sense to him, and although he'd already decided that he was on this ride until the end, he prayed to the unfair God above to help him continue to find the right words to comfort her while on that ride.

Eliza came out of the chicken coop with a basket of eggs, just as they were approaching, surprising her as well as them. Typically, she collected the eggs for the food shelf early in the morning, before anyone at the farm was up and moving. Old Man wondered if that wasn't to avoid the uncomfortable conversations they had about Wife at times, or because of her busy schedule. Either way, it was fine by him.

Eliza stands no taller than five feet, and that's pushing it. She was a few years behind Wife and Old Man in school, and was a pest even then, following them wherever they went. She still wore her hair exactly the same way as she did as a kid, dirty brown and cut in a short bob. The only difference being the random specks of gray. At age sixty-eight she was still a cute little thing, even if she was fairly round. Her chubby red cheeks a clue to her high blood pressure and a truly busy life.

She was a good woman, would do anything for anyone…except shut up when you needed her to. She volunteered at church, the food shelf and prepared lunch seven days a week at the soup kitchen in downtown Ottumwa, all out of the goodness in her heart. But, she was also a bossy and opinionated woman, one who was still lucky enough to catch a husband.

The problem was that she made it clear to Old Man every chance she got that Wife should be in a nursing home, because he couldn't possibly care for her the way she needed to be cared for. This hurt him, and he

47

resented it deeply.

She didn't understand that the farm was the one thing Wife still knew, and he wasn't about to take that away from her. He knew that moving her to an unfamiliar place would be the end of what was left of her and as long as he was alive, that was not going to happen. No matter what anyone thought.

The subject of how to deal with Wife's deterioration was one Eliza brought up, no matter where they happened to run into each other, which is the biggest reason he avoided taking Wife into town. The sympathy, and or judgment, he detected only made things harder on him. The conversation was the same, always the same, and inevitably both of them walked away from each other frustrated.

She just didn't get it, and wouldn't shut up about it. He no longer had the energy to debate the issue with her, which is why they were both better off not having these forced conversations. It somehow took something real away from the hundreds if not thousands of great ones they'd had over the years.

"Oh hi, Hugh", she said, looking over at Wife and setting the basket full of eggs on the hood of her car.

"Hey, Betty, how you doing, honey? Eliza said to Wife. "Mom says, we have to do our chores before she gets home", Wife suddenly added, turning Eliza's curious expression into an ugly twist of horror.

Here we go again, Old Man thought to himself.

"Oh my God, Hugh, are you alright? Is everything here alright?" She said, wiping her hands on her pants, but never taking her eyes off of Wife. Old Man noticed, as she began her campaign of saving the world, that her red lipstick was smeared all over her top teeth. It distracted him briefly, which was kind of nice. He chuckled at his private joke, but answered, "Yes Eliza, everything here is just peachy. How's everything with you?"

She nervously ran her tongue over her teeth, as if sensing his private joke.

"Fine", she managed to get out. "How's Betty, Hugh? I mean, how is she, really?"

He sighed heavily. "Eliza, as you know, my wife is not well. That hasn't changed, but other than that she's fine, really", he said, trying not to sound as exasperated as he felt. Then he changed the subject "Today's a big day for us, isn't it dear?" Hugging Wife, he went on. "Eileen and Jacob are moving to the farm and we have a lot to do to get ready, so if you'll excuse us?"

Done with Eliza, he turned Wife around towards the barn.

48

"I heard they were moving in", Eliza said to his backside. "I'm real happy to hear that Hugh, happy for all of you", she poured her round body into her car, but before she drove away she rolled down the window and hollered, "By the way, Hugh, there's an ugly little bird trapped in the coop with your chickens. It's in a nest with one of them for goodness sake! I had to push the darn thing out of the way just to get at an egg. I was afraid I was going to get pecked to death! Just thought I should let you know."

Then she drove away. "Like the wicked witch of the West, or was it the East? Old Man muttered aloud. He smiled at her comments. Like a bird no bigger than her hand could peck her to death. "I didn't know Eliza was such a pansy", he said out loud as they walked in through the barn doors. "How about you woman? Did you know Eliza was a pansy?"

CRITTERS

There was no response, which was just fine. He already knew the answer anyway.

After double checking that the barn was ready for what was to come, Old Man led Wife back out of the barn and headed for the coop, to check on the "killer bird."

By then, the chickens were heading out of the building, anticipating the food that soon would be scattered all around.

He led Wife into the coop and sat her down on the shelf, but when she made no move to look in the box for her Boy, he did. The box was empty. He searched the small building with his eyes until he found the bird sitting on a two-by-four overhead.

Old Man felt an odd sense of relief, but didn't point the bird out to her. Instead, he put a large bit in the drill and began drilling a couple of holes the size of a half dollar through the front of building. When that was finished, he stood back a couple of feet to make sure the holes were big enough for a bird to get through. Then he went outside and gathered up a few sticks and brought them inside. He pulled out his pocket knife and sat down on the shelf next to Wife to whittle the two short sticks smooth and just to the right length. Picking up the drill again, he drilled two more holes in the wall, but this time tiny, shallow holes. After placing the sticks tightly in the holes, he turned to Wife and asked if she thought her Boy would like them.

Before she could react to the magic word, he heard the roar of a truck engine coming down the driveway and park, making him grab at Wife's arm too fast for comfort.

"No!" She said, with clear meaning and an equally negative look.

"Okay, you can stay here, but I'll be right outside", he said, hurrying out of the coop.

Getting out of the large truck were Chod and Dude Kremer, Fara's younger brothers. Old Man had always assumed that Chod and Dude were nicknames, but had never known them by any other names. There had been a third boy in their family, named Chicory, like the coffee. Everyone called him Chick for short. He died in a farm accident when he was seven.

"Morning boys", he said to the sixty something gentle giants who came around the front of the truck with warm smiles and strong hand-shakes to greet him.

These men had been young boys when their parents were killed in a car accident. Fara, who was in tenth grade at the time, dropped out of school to raise them and take over the duties of the farm. Not only did she raise these boys, but she turned them into fine men along the way.

Together, the three of them built one of the largest cattle businesses in the state of Iowa, remaining honest and humble throughout, which Old Man believed to be remarkable. He admired them to no end.

Old Man could hear the young animals kicking the inside of the truck bed in protest. Eager for a first look, he walked around to the back of the truck to peek through the wooden side rails, just to make sure they hadn't brought him bulls by mistake.

Grinning, he said, "I think we'll put 'em in the yard for a while, let 'em calm down some. I don't want them kicking down the stalls I just rebuilt."

"Good idea, Hugh", Chod said, smiling, then added, "Fara's right be-hind us with the hay."

"Well then, I'd better get busy and put some coffee on. I know how Fara's gotta have her caffeine.." They all laughed, then Old Man said, "Just give me a couple of minutes guys."

The two men watched as Old Man disappeared into the chicken coop, reappearing seconds later with Betty in tow.

"Hi there, Betty Lou", Dude said as he slowly walked over and placed a large hand on her shoulder. Betty Lou was one of those childhood nicknames that stuck with her like glue, connecting her forever with the people of her past.

Wife stood at attention, as the wheels in her head struggled to turn. Her eyes searched Dude's face for something familiar, then she turned and did the same with Chod.

Out of respect, no one said a word while the woman struggled in front of them. They knew she had trouble. After a few minutes of this, Wife tugged on Old Man's arm, letting him know that she was ready to move on.

They began walking towards the house, when Dude hollered, "Take your time, Hugh. We'll unload those crazy critters." A deep hearty laugh followed, fading away as he and Wife entered the kitchen.

Old Man sat Wife down at the table while he brewed a pot of coffee for Fara. The rich aroma filled the otherwise stale air in the house. He stood at the window and watched the boys back the truck up to the gate. He wanted to be out there with them something terrible. Then he watched as another truck stacked with hay bales drove in and parked in front of the barn. The driver's door opened and out from behind the wheel came Fara, with her pipe hanging out of one side of her mouth. He watched her jump down from the truck like she was a kid, and then almost lose her balance when her feet hit the ground. "Stubborn old coot", he said out loud.

FARA, THE RIGHT STUFF

He was so excited that he paced the floor, waiting for the coffee to finish brewing, when Fara walked in through the door like she owned the place. The men's coveralls she wore were rolled up at the ankles, exposing her small work boots. On top of a thick head of gray hair was her signature red hat. Rarely was her goofy outfit's void of that red hat.

You would never have guessed by looking at her that this solid little woman was nearing eighty. Her crooked fingers could still split an apple in half. Something she did often to entertain the young men at the church BBQ's, betting five dollars per apple then gloating with a sly glance in their direction the following Sunday as she dropped the money into the passing donation plate.

Fara never married, but everyone from around these parts knew she'd been in love. They knew she loved a man that she could never have, a man she'd met doing business at the cattle auctions, a married man who was a professional in both business and empty promises. Why she hung in there with him for all of those years, only she could say. Their affair lasted thirty years before he got killed in a car accident, along with his wife and two teenage daughters. A train hit their car one spring morning, splitting it in half and leaving debris and four lifeless bodies along the iron tracks and sprouting fields.

It was the only time in all the years that Old Man had known Fara for her to ask for anything. She sought them, him and Wife out on that day,. She needing to be away from town and all of the eyes that bored into her broken soul. It was painful to watch a strong person like Fara fall apart, it made her friends feel inadequate and helpless. All she wanted when she arrived was a safe place to be with her anger and her grief, so Old Man and Wife walked her out into the blooming prairie, and stood quietly at her side for hours, watching as she vacillated between heart wrenching grief and fits of anger. They cringed every time she screamed, "fuck", the mother of all swear words over the vast landscape until her voice was hoarse and her body limp with exhaustion.

Then, without saying a word, Fara stuck her pipe in her mouth, took a hold of each of their hands and squeezed. Not letting go, she led them back to her truck, where she climbed in and drove away.

Everyone had known about the affair, but no one talked about it, at least not that Old Man had ever heard. Nor did he or Wife ever ask about it, before or after the accident. They figured it was none of their business.

Old Man remembers feeling honored, however, that she'd come to them with her crazy rampage. He was honored that she trusted them, honored that she chose their fields to scream at like a drunken sailor.

Looking over at her now, Old Man smiled at the memory. "You tough old bird you", he said to the woman who was now seated next to Wife, waiting for her cup of coffee.

"Takes one to know one buddy", she said, as Old Man sat the steaming cup down in front of her.

"How you doing girl?" Fara asked, reaching over and touching Betty's frail hand lying motionless on the table. Then, pointing out the window, "You see them calves out there honey? They're wild ones. I couldn't wait to get 'em off my hands, that's for damn sure", she said, smiling over at Old Man and adding a wink when he joined them at the table.

Wife turned and looked out the window, then back again at Fara. She was silent, but responded with a smile each time Fara spoke.

Though one couldn't tell by looking at her, Fara was worth millions of dollars, as were her brothers. Years of hard work and good decisions paid off for these small-town kids who'd become wealthy on their own sweat and tears.

When her lover died, she was as shocked as everyone else to find out that he had willed his Cement Company to her. It was a successful business that generated big money, which she used to keep hundreds of people in this small town employed, as well as creating more jobs by building Silver Woods, the assisted living complex in Ottumwa. She donating it as a not-for-profit once it was off its feet and running.

She set up a trust for the public schools in Ottumwa, so they would always be able to purchase new buses and improvements when needed. She did the same with the food shelf, keeping it always in food, including delivering fresh meat from her ranch once every month. She even started the very first Meals on Wheels program in Wapello County. There was no question that her wealth gave her loss some purpose.

She is known by the local kids, even the grown up ones, as 'Aunt Fara,' which she considers the highest honor of her life, and although it is true that she drinks and swears like a sailor on leave, never do you hear an ill word spoken about the woman in the red hat.

After a couple of cups of coffee and some updating, Fara rose and walked around the table to where Wife sat. "Come on old girl, let's go see what the guys are up to out there."

Fara took a hold of Wife and stood her up, then laced her fingers in Wife's and walked her out of the house, just like that. Old Man remained at the table for a minute, reflecting on their long friendship, and then took the time before joining the rest to apologize to the not so unfair God above for his fluctuating faith.

Once outside, he found everyone standing around the fence watching the two little calves work the devil out of themselves by running around the yard just as Eileen and Jacob pulled in.

The car had barely come to a complete stop when Jacob opened the door and came running up to the fence. "Two of them! Oh Grandpa, two of them! They're perfect, thank you! Thank you, thank you!" He said, hugging Old Man.

Thoroughly enjoying the happiness pouring out of his grandson, and the warmth of his short arms around his waist, he reluctantly took a hold of the scrawny arms, pulling him just far enough away that he could look down at the excited boy.

"Jacob, these calves are a gift from Aunt Fara, so it's her you need to thank." With that, Jacob immediately released his grip on his Grandpa and ran over to the fence, where Fara leaned, and hugged her tight. "Thank you ,Aunt Fara", he said. After a couple of minutes, she peeled him off of her and looked into his teary eyes

"Okay, boy, now this is some serious business you've got going on here. Those four-legged creatures are not toys, ya' hear? You got to take care, real good care, of them. You understand?"

"I will Aunt Fara, I promise. I love them so much already!" He said, backing away from her with his head down towards the ground. He began to walk away, making like he was going to walk right past Chod and Dude, when he grabbed Chod and gave him a quick squeeze, then did the same with Dude, surprising them both.

Eager to get in the yard with his new little buddies, he started walking back to the gate, passing his Grandma on the way. She stood alone and silent near a fence post, watching the calves. All eyes were still on him when he did a 180-degree turn and took a hold of his Grandma by the waist. He said nothing, just hung onto her. They watched Wife's limp arms come alive, leaving her side and circling Jacob's little shoulders and neck. Then she rested her head on top of his for the longest time.

It was a tender moment, which brought tears to the eyes of all in the captive audience. After a few minutes, Fara broke the silence. "I'm not getting any younger. So, let's get our asses in gear and get that hay unloaded before winter shows up!"

Trading the tears for laughter, they all got busy.

It was late afternoon by the time the Kremers said their goodbyes, leaving only a few good hours of daylight to unload the car and trailer stuffed with Eileen's and Jacob's things.

Old Man sat Wife in a weathered wicker chair near the kitchen door, where she could watch the comings and goings, which she did. She made eye contact each time they passed by, and greeted them with a "hello" as if each time was the first. The three of them returned her greetings, never tiring of the number of times they said it. They were all having fun.

When the car and trailer were completely empty, Eileen announced that it was time for supper. Old Man and Jacob high-fived each other in triumph for the good day's work, and in anticipation of filling their bellies with something yummy.

Having assumed the day would be a long one, Eileen had stopped at the local Kentucky Fried Chicken before heading out to the farm, purchasing a huge bucket of chicken, a tub of coleslaw, and biscuits with honey, all of which was consumed by all at warp speed.

Not surprisingly, the only one with any energy left was Jacob. "Can I put the calves in the barn now mom?" Jacob asked, pushing his chair away from the table.

Eileen looked over to Old Man for input. He nodded 'yes,' but added, "I'll be out in a minute to help you bud. Locking that gate is tricky; I want to make sure you see how I do it. We don't want your girls to get loose now, do we?"

"No, we sure don't, Grandpa. Okay, I'll just fart around outside and wait for you", he said.

"Sounds good", Old Man said, chuckling at Jacob's choice of words, and watched him skip through the kitchen and disappear through the door.

Eileen offered to change Wife's clothes, and get her ready for bed so he could get outside before it got too dark.

"There'll be plenty of time for that, honey. Thanks for the offer, but I'll take care of it", he said, offering her a smile filled with warmth and gratitude.

Once Old Man had given Wife a bath, he changed her into her night-clothes, then sat her down in that familiar worn leather chair. From there she could watch the sun lower itself behind the large oak, or watch Eileen clean up in the kitchen.

He knew Eileen was capable of taking care of Wife, and anything else for that matter, yet he thought it a good idea that she observe their routine before diving into the care taking duties.

Routines were necessary. He'd come to understand how necessary they were to a person who was lost most of their waking hours. He also had no intention of giving up his duties completely. Wife wasn't the only one who needed routine.

Out in the barn, Old Man and Jacob successfully secured the calves into their new stalls, then fed and watered them when he turned to Jacob and asked, "Have you thought about what you are going to name them son?"

Immediately, Jacob pointed to the larger one with spots. It was obvious he had been thinking about it. "That one is Daisy, and I think I'll call the black one Charlotte", Jacob answered.

"How would you feel about calling the black one Bob?" Old Man suggested.

Laughing, Jacob said, "Bob's a boy's name, Grandpa." "Duh", he added.

Old Man returned the "duh" with a large smile. "Once upon a time your dad had a bull named Bob, did you know that?" Jacob raised his eyebrows and shook his head. "Your dad and your Grandma loved him, more than any of the other critters on the farm, and that's saying a lot, because they loved all of the critters. I was thinking about how your Grandma might just like to have another Bob around this place. But it's up to you. Whatever you name them is okay with me. Just think about it."

GRANDMA

Jacob sat down on a bucket and leaned his forehead against the stall so he could watch the calves through the slits in the wood. Changing the subject, he asked, "What's wrong with Grandma anyway?"

Old Man sucked in a big breath and let it out slowly. "Well son, your Grandma has a disease called dementia. It's a disease that slowly takes away your memories. You know that game you play on your thingama-jig, PacMan?" Jacob nodded. "Well, imagine those little guys cruising around in a brain, eating everything in their path as they go along. It's kind of like that. Does that make any sense?"

Jacob gasped, but nodded again. "That's awful", he said, looking up at his Grandpa.

"Yes it is son, it's worse than awful. Most days she doesn't even talk, or seem to know who I am. And she's only going to get worse, so don't be surprised when your Grandma does or says things that seem a little weird."

"Like what?" Jacob asked.

"Well, let's see. For example, um, she might think you are your dad at times, or even that you are someone else entirely. She's been going back and forth lately, between being a little girl to being a young mother. What is left of her memory seems to be of the past, long ago stuff. Very little of her memory is of anything or anyone recent. More than likely, honey, she doesn't even know that you exist. I don't think she can remember that your dad grew up and became a man, or that he died, which is a blessing in a way. It's hard to explain, but no matter what your Grandma says or does, it's really important that you not be afraid of her, you hear me?"

Old Man stroked Jacob's face.

"I could go on son, but I think you get the point. Her train runs off its tracks and has a hard time getting back on." To lighten the mood, he added, "Just the other day, I heard her answer the phone, and when I walked into the room she was holding that statue of Roy Rogers to her ear, and talking into it!" Old Man's lips formed a crooked smile just remembering the sight of that. Jacob smiled too.

"I'm not afraid of Grandma", Jacob said. "I think she's funny, and besides, I love her." Jacob declared.

"You sweet thing, she loves you too. Just remember that trapped inside of her is the same wonderful person we have always known."

Then Old Man's head turned upward towards the hay loft and his eyes searched beyond the rafters for the invisible presence of God. Then whispered "thank you."

When his eyes returned to Jacob, he found him standing right next to him, empathy and understanding reflected on his young face. Old Man couldn't help but grab hold of the boy and give him a kiss on the head.

"Okay, that's enough of that", he said, choking back tears, and releasing him. "Now before we call it quits for the night, there's someone I want you to meet."

On their way out of the barn, Jacob said, "Bob's a good name for the black one Grandpa."

With a smile pasted on Old Man's face, he and his grandson made their way to the chicken coop. The night was blissfully quiet, and the oncoming winter rode on the breeze. Old Man was ready for winter now, in fact he was ready for anything that came his way.

"Who the heck am I going to meet in the chicken coop Grandpa?" Jacob asked, as they entered the small building.

"You'll see in a minute boy", was Old Man's reply, and he chuckled. "Boy, meets boy", he thought to himself.

It was nearly too dark inside the coop to see anything, so Old Man pulled on the string that hung from the bulb on the wall, illuminating the space in a yellowish glow.

He peeked into Boy's box and started laughing hard when he saw Mrs. Nickels asleep in it. She lazily opened one eye and looked up at him.

"What the devil are you doing in here?" He asked the groggy cat.

Curious, Jacob climbed up on the shelf and looked inside the box. "I can't believe the chickens let her sleep in here Grandpa.."

"Me either", Old man murmured, busily looking in the rest of the boxes until he found what he was looking for in a box on the top shelf, next to a nesting chicken.

"Looky here Jacob? This is who I wanted you to meet. Let me introduce you to, Boy."

Old Man stepped away, so Jacob could get a good look in the box. "That looks like the same bird Mrs. Nickels had in her mouth the other day", Jacob said, looking at Old Man with a questioning expression and an exaggerated twist of his lips.

"That's the one. Your Grandma and I found him a couple of weeks ago out in the yard. He hit the window and, oh..it's a long story.

Your Grandma took a liking to it, so I kept it for her. She calls him Boy." Then Old Man raised his shoulders and put his palms up, as if to say that it didn't make sense to him either. "The little guy seems to like it in here, though" he said.

"That's crazy", Jacob said, still looking at the bird that appeared to be looking back at him.

"Which part son? It's all crazy if you ask me. What I can't believe is that Mrs. Nickels hasn't made a meal out the little guy yet, and I sure hope she doesn't. I'm getting kind of used to having him around. So, Boy here is now your responsibility too, and since the bugs will be gone soon, you will need to keep some birdseed in here for him eat."

"Okay", was all Jacob could manage to say.

Before Jacob climbed down from the shelf to join his Grandpa though, he reached over and patted Mrs. Nickels on the head. "Now you leave Boy alone ya' hear? He ordered the cat. Then they walked out of the coop and into the house, like what just happened was as normal as apple pie on Sunday.

It was quiet when they entered the house. Kentucky Fried Chicken aroma still hung in the air, and the only lights on were the ones over the kitchen sink and the empty chair, where Wife no longer rested. It felt cozy.

Old Man was just about to tell Jacob to get ready for bed, when Eileen came down from the second-floor bedroom.

"I thought you guys got lost out there", she said, smiling and holding an armful of empty boxes. "What were you up to for so long?"

"Just getting the critters settled in for the night, is all", Jacob said, just a bit defensively.

"Oh", his mom said, giving them both a quizzical look.

"I put Betty to bed a while ago, but made sure she was asleep before I went upstairs to unpack. Almost got it done too, so tomorrow I will start on Jacob's room."

"That's great", Old Man said as his stomach did a flip. He worried that Eileen might not have kept an eye on Wife while so engaged in unpacking. This is why he wasn't going to turn over his duties entirely. He couldn't risk losing Wife ever again. But he knew Eileen meant well, she always meant well.

He hurried to the bedroom, hoping his fear wasn't too obvious, but when he peeked inside the dark room, he saw the lump on the bed and heard a soft snore. All was well.

"Thank you", he said, walking back towards the kitchen "I'm sorry we weren't around to help you unpack. Right Jacob?" He said, nudging the boy with his elbow.

"Yeah, me too mom, dang it", Jacob said with a grin.

"Okay, time for bed, young man. We can start all over again tomorrow.

Now git", Eileen ordered, pushing Jacob gently toward his new room.

"Night mom, night Grandpa, and thanks for everything!" Jacob said with a wink, before disappearing into his room.

"What was that all about?" Eileen asked, having noticed the conspiratorial wink.

"You got me", Old Man answered, shrugging his shoulders. "All I know is that it's time I hit the hay too. See you in the morning, honey."

But before he reached his bedroom, he turned and looked at his daughter-in-law. "And thank you again for everything!"

The next morning, Old Man panicked when looked over and found the space next to him empty. The lump in the bed was gone, and fear grabbed hold of him once again. He tore his robe off the chair as he ran out of the room, calling her name "Wife?" He ran into the living room and called again. "Wife?" Before he got to the kitchen, he was stopped dead in his tracks by the singing that floated down the stairs. It was coming from the bedroom that was now Eileen's, but it wasn't Eileen's voice he heard. It was Wife's.

He took the stairs two at a time until reaching the doorway to the bedroom. He froze in place when he saw her sitting on the bed, cradling a doll in her arms and singing the song she had been humming for weeks.

"You are my sunshine, my only sunshine, you make me happy when skies are gray", she sang. Then she reverted back to humming a few verses, until she got to, "Please don't take my sunshine away", which she belted out, more like a desperate plea than a song. Wife held the doll near her face, until she finally looked over to Old Man, then held it out for him to see. "See"?" she asked, but after a few seconds she tucked it back up against her chest, and continued rocking back and forth. "Boy", she said, smiling down at the worn cloth doll.

He was so relieved that she wasn't wandering around outside that he didn't know whether to laugh or to cry, but he definitely felt like he could do either.

BABY BOY

When he sat down on the edge of the bed next to her, Wife immediately reached over and took one of his hands, and placed it on the doll.

"Boy", she said again, making a point, or an introduction, he wasn't sure which. Then she went back to humming.

He nudged in a little closer, placing his free arm around her thin shoulders, until their bodies touched and he could feel her warmth. Tears filled his eyes, spilling over and running down his cheeks "Yes, Wife. Boy", he said.

At that moment, all he wanted to do was assure the woman sitting next to him that he would never take her sunshine away, ever. But there was no point in telling her that, and he knew it.

Eileen came running up the stairs with Jacob right behind her, sounding like a herd of elephants, which gave Old Man enough leeway to wipe the tears from his face. Eileen hesitated at the doorway, evaluating the scene before taking a few short steps into the room. A sleepy Jacob remained where he was.

She bent down and dug into one of her boxes, and when her hand came out of the box it held a little plastic baby bottle. She looked at Old Man with compassion before handing the bottle to Wife, who eagerly accepted it and began feeding the doll.

"I'll go make some breakfast. You guys come on down when you're ready, okay?" Eileen said.

Old Man stared at the empty doorway, listening to the sound of their bare feet on the wooden stairs. He felt appreciation for how Eileen jumped right in and went along with Wife, no matter what. He also appreciated the sound of feet on the stairs. It had been a long time since he heard that sound.

He looked over at his woman, his partner and friend of a lifetime, the mother of their only child, and saw something in her face that he hadn't seen in a very long time, peace.

Only when his arm started to grow numb did he lower it from her shoulders, down to her waist, and move Wife and 'child' off the bed towards the stairs.

Rays from the early morning sun darted in and out of the dirty window as they passed it. By the time they crested the top step, the wonderful smell of sausage and cakes found them. They entered the kitchen just as Eileen had finished filling their plates. Old Man sat Wife down at the table, and walked back to Eileen "Thank you", he said just above a whisper.

"No need for that Hugh", she said, looking into his tear-filled eyes. "I get it, I really do, and it's going to be alright. Trust me."

"I do trust you honey, and I'm so damned glad you're here I can hardly stand it", he said, as Jacob walked into the room wearing an old pair of Charly's pants. They were so big on him that it was hard not to laugh, and laugh they did. It's true that timing is everything.

As Eileen set the plates on the table, Old Man walked over to the hall closet and pulled out a pair of suspenders, and attached them to his grandson's trousers.

"There boy, now you look like a real farmer", he said.

"Awesome", Jacob said, admiring himself in the full-length mirror attached to the closet door.

"Now, let's join Grandma and her Boy at the table."

Hearing that, Wife looked up and smiled. It was going to be a great day. Old Man could feel it.

BOY

I have no complaints, other than the furry one taking over my nest. This is turning out to be not such a bad place to spend the winter. Sure beats the cramped hole of a tree, or the usual tangle of musty grass.

In fact, the other night when the wind blew in through the cracks, my bed partner even made sure I was safe and warm all night.

I have plenty to eat, a nest to sleep in - even if I do have to share it - knowing now that I have friends that will protect me if I need, makes me feel pretty darn good.

I'm even fairly certain that the furry one has joined my team, if you know what I mean.

Wife hasn't been to see me for a while, but a short little guy has. Now if I can figure out who that short little guy is, I can put my fears to rest for a few more months.

ANOTHER CLOSE CALL

During breakfast, Jacob looked over at his mom, wondering why they hadn't gone to church like they usually do on Sundays. He wanted to ask, but was afraid that if he brought it up she would make them go, and the plans he had for the day would be ruined.

He was eager to get outside and get his chores done so he could spend the rest of the day with his new calves. He hurried through his stack of pancakes and decided to keep his curiosity about church to himself, when suddenly his Grandma started to choke on a bite of sausage.

Eileen jumped up and ran around the table to Wife. "Betty, are you alright?" She cried, patting Wife's back hard. Then she put two fingers in Wife's mouth to feel for what blocked her airway. Wife's eyes bulged from their sockets as they stared into the eyes of the woman who had her fingers down her throat.

Old Man stood up, but didn't know what to do. "What should I do? What should I do Eileen!?" Old Man cried.

"Please try to stay calm Hugh", she said, removing her fingers from Wife's mouth. "I know CPR."

Still seated, Jacob watched in horror as his grandmother's face turned a faint shade of purple, then watched as his mother stood her up and moved behind her, in order to perform the Heimlich maneuver which scared him even more.

After a few pulls on Wife's little abdomen, out flew a chunk of Jimmy Dean sausage, landing on the linoleum floor with a thud. Just then Mrs. Nickels appeared out of nowhere and took care of that in a hurry.

Within seconds of having her life saved by the daughter in law she no longer recognized, Wife was back down in her chair, rocking and humming to her Boy, as if nothing had happened.

Old Man felt angry at being so helpless, and not knowing what to do. Eileen sensed by the pain written on his face.

"Hugh, help me out with the dishes would you?" Eileen asked, walking away without waiting for an answer. Looking out of the window as she placed the dirty dishes in the sink, she didn't look at Old Man when he came in and stood next to her.

"Thank God, you knew what to do", he said. "I can't help thinking about what would have happened if you hadn't been here."

Searching for the right words to say to him, words that would calm and re-assure him that everything was going to be alright, she said, "Hugh, you can't know how to do everything. I'm trained in CPR and that's part of why I'm here. Come on, we're a team now, remember?" She said, turning away from the window to face him, his tall lanky frame towering next to her.

"Hugh, when I was in college, one of the things I had to study was the different types of diseases and how they attack, not only animals, but people too. I studied the brain and all of the things that can cripple it. Dementia and Alzheimer's are two of the diseases I studied. So did Charly. He was in most of my classes, that's actually when we started to date."

She smiled after sharing that with him, and so did Old Man, but his fear-filled expression didn't change. "I don't claim to be an expert", she continued. "But I do remember a few things that I'd like to tell you about. Okay with you?"

He nodded.

"For example, some people with dementia wander. It's a trait of this disease, a trait I didn't realize Betty had until recently. So, I promise you from here on out, that I'll be much more aware of where Betty is when I'm alone with her."

Fearing Eileen was feeling guilty herself, Old Man started to say something, but Eileen plunged ahead. "I also know that choking is something that happens in the later stages of this disease. It's a sign that she no longer remembers to chew her food."

Old Man backed up a few feet, but never took his eyes off of her. "In nursing homes, when a patient gets to this point, they puree their food, so maybe that's something we should begin doing. I also know that some women, the ones who were mothers, go through a period where they search for their children. As they regress in age, so do their memories of people in their lives, particularly the children. So they search. When I saw Betty with my old doll, I knew right away what it represented to her. That's why I gave her the baby bottle."

Eileen smiled. Then she went on, cautiously. "A few days ago, when I was cleaning out Charly's room, I found some photos of him. When Betty saw them, I could tell that she recognized him. She pointed to him in each photo and called him, 'Boy.'"

Old Man nodded, confirming that what she was telling him was something he was already aware of.

Eileen continued. "When I heard her call that bird the same name, I put two and two together. She's searching for something in her past, a time when she was a mother, a time when she took care of someone, or something, like her son or the animals on the farm."

He understood what she was saying, and didn't disagree. When she finished talking, the two of them just stood at the counter, looking out the window. "Just remember this, Old Man", she said, breaking their silence. "We can handle anything as a team. Anything." Their foreheads came together and touched, sealing the deal.

"Mom?" Jacob said, coming into the kitchen and abruptly ending the private moment.

"Yes, son?"

"Didn't you used to sing that same song to me? The one Grandma's humming?"

"I sure did honey. Do you want me to sing it to you right now?"

"No way Jose! All I want to do is go outside!" He said, as he headed for the door. "I'm going to feed the chickens, Grandpa, and anything else that's living in there."

And he gave his grandfather a sly wink. "I'll be in the barn."

"I'll be out in a few minutes", Old Man said, winking back. But the boy was long gone by then.

By the time Jacob got to the coop, the chickens were already outside, pecking at the bare ground. He couldn't wait to see who, or what, was in the coop, and was disappointed when he found it empty. As instructed, he placed birdseed in the window sill, then searched the small building one more time. Still finding no sign of Boy, he went about the chore of cleaning out the poop, replacing it with sawdust and a little straw. Then he hurriedly scattered the feed for the hungry chickens, and took off running towards the barn, tripping on the pant legs made for someone else, someone much taller and bigger than he was.

He noticed Mrs. Nickels perched on top of a nearby fence post, watching him, and walked over to her.

"Good morning, Mrs. Nickels", he said, as he stroked her head and then her silky body. The cat's tail flipped back and forth in pleasure. "I sure hope you didn't eat that little bird for breakfast, Jacob said, "Or you're in some deep shit." Then, he continued on to the barn.

Inside the house, Old Man sat at the table with a fresh cup of tea, watching Wife happily rock her baby Boy.

Eileen grabbed her cup of coffee off of the counter and joined them, saying, "You know, Thanksgiving's right around the corner. How would you feel about inviting a few people out to the farm? Make it a real old fashion Thanksgiving?"

It had been a long time since Old Man and Wife celebrated a real Thanksgiving meal, much less entertained dinner guests. The thought of it warmed him.

November did that to people. The skies changed, the air changed, and darkness slowly took over the light. Barren fields transformed themselves into stages, with snow-covered fields revealing the tracks of what lived and traveled across the landscape.

Old Man asked, "What do think, Wife? Want to invite some people out here for Thanksgiving?"

Her blue eyes flickered with life, but there was no response.

He didn't mind. The flicker was enough for him, and suddenly he became aware of all of the things he was thankful for. His expression answered Eileen's question.

He gave Eileen's arm a little squeeze. "Sounds like a wonderful idea honey. Tell me what you want me to do."

"All I want you to do is get that barrel stove in the barn working, and leave the rest to me. I'm so excited Hugh, it's going to be the best Thanksgiving ever!"

He was happy to see Eileen happy. A gathering of people they loved and the idea of a true Thanksgiving feast might just be what the doctor ordered.

Old Man led Wife to the chair by the window, as he did every morning for more months than he could count. But this time she refused to sit down. When he tried to bend her at the waist, she stiffened and straightened her crooked body. This was new. Puzzled, he bent down and looked into her eyes, hoping they would give him a clue as to where she was. When he did, she returned his look, mocking him, then she started to laugh. He couldn't help but laugh himself.

"You think this is funny, do you"? He asked, still trying to bend her stiff frame into the chair.

"Yes", she answered.

Shocked, Old Man let go of her, but then quickly grabbed her back again and held her against his chest. He justified his quick movements with the knowledge that the moment of familiarity was already evaporating.

Wife's arms were trapped against his belly. As he ate up their closeness, she tried to pull away, so he released his grip and backed up. Wife pointed to the bundle of cloth she cradled in one arm, but said nothing. Her eyes and pointing finger said it all. She was worried that they were going to crush the baby. She was still in this world with him - sort of - which amazed him.

"Oh, of course, the Boy. I'm sorry", he said, stroking the bundle she now held out for him to see. Old Man could hardly contain the tangle of emotions running through him. He glanced over at the table where Eileen sat. She offered no assistance, as it was clear to her that none was needed. Instead, she looked back at him, grinning, both amused and touched.

Old Man turned back to Wife and said, "Let's go see how Daisy and Bob are doing on this fine morning, shall we?" He placed a sweater over her shoulders and led her out of the house.

Still grinning, Eileen got up and poured herself another cup of coffee, and then began making the guest list for their Thanksgiving dinner.

Outside, Old Man and Wife strolled through the maze of pecking chickens, and he noticed that she took no interest in the chicken coop as they passed. So, they continued down the lane towards the barn, passing Mrs. Nickels. The cat sat motionless on a post, watching the nearby open field, ready to pounce on the slightest of movement.

Wife also paid no attention to the cat who hunted like a hawk, perched on a post, but Old Man did. He couldn't help himself, and greeted their old friend with a "hello." The preoccupied cat ignored them.

They left the daylight and entered the dim and dusty light of the barn, where a sweet little voice was coming from one of the stalls.

"You are my sunshine, my only sunshine."

Old Man stopped and listened to the sweetness, and so did Wife.

"You make me happy when skies are gray. You'll never know dear…."

Right then, Wife broke away from Old Man and walked towards the stall, where Jacob was sitting on the ground with his arm around the calf named Daisy and joined in the singing, not missing a beat.

"…how much I love you. Please don't take my sunshine away."

Jacob looked up at his grandmother and smiled. She smiled back at him, and right then something came fluttering down from the rafters and landed on Wife's shoulder. It was Boy, the bird.

Old Man stood alone watching as the crazy miracle unfolded before him, knowing that no matter how hard he tried, he would never be able to describe it to anyone.

One more time, he found himself searching past the rafters for the invisible presence he held so much faith in. He knew right then that the ones he really wanted to share the miracles with had already witnessed, if not handed them to him.

The rest of the day was spent outside, with no more sign of Boy. After they brought the calves out to the yard, he flew away to do whatever it was birds do. Old Man cleaned out the wood stove in the barn, as requested by Eileen. He hauled firewood into the barn with his four-wheeler and cart, until there was enough wood to stay the winter.

Wife and baby rode on the seat in front of him, while he worked and, even though there was heat in the autumn sun, the air was still cool.

Every once in a while, Old Man reached around in front of Wife to wipe her runny nose with his hanky. He added one of his flannel shirts to her sweater to make sure she stayed warm and toasty. One of his biggest fears was wife getting sick with fever.

He remembered how afraid he was when the year before she was sick with a cold and high fever. He took her to town to see Doctor Spevak, and before they left his office with instructions, advice and plenty of antibiotics, he pulled Old Man aside, out of earshot of Wife.

"You know what we call pneumonia in the old and the sick, Hugh? We call it the old man's friend. Do you know what I mean by that?"

He did know. Doc was saying that dying in your sleep from pneumonia isn't the worst thing that can happen to a person who is slowly dying anyway. He was saying that it was a blessing to those who suffer from whatever is it that brutally steals their life away from them.

66

Hugh hoped instead that God would take her away when the time came, but not by a fever which he had the choice to treat or not to treat. Even though the truth of it was, that at one time he'd considered taking both of their lives, die together, then neither of them would be left alone.

He wasn't certain at that time that Wife was true suffering; failing fast, yes, but not suffering. Hell, he was suffering, but no one was talking about him.

It was her fate that was being broached by the doctor; a man he'd known since the man was a boy in elementary school and in 4H. Hell, Wife and Old Man had even attended doc's high school graduation ceremony.

Old Man trusted this man, cared for him even, but he was not ready or willing to talk about 'letting her die.'

"I hear what you are saying, Doc, but she's not ready, and I'm not ready to talk about it, okay? I'll call you if she needs any more antibiotics. Thank you." Old Man said as he guided his wife through the through the office doors.

"Take care Hugh, you too Betty Lou" the doctor said watching the two bent frames slowly walk out of the clinic.

Faith led him through that next few months - faith and love, and the fear of being without her would dictate his days.

Remembering all this and enjoying the feel now of her back warm against him as they rode, he felt her heart beat on his chest. She hadn't said another word since joining Jacob in 'you are my sunshine' that morning, and for the first time in a long time, the silence was beautiful.

They hadn't been this kind of close in years. It was the best of the best. As he soaked it up, he promised himself that from that day forward, if any words came from her mouth, no matter how mixed up, they would be a gift he would not take for granted. Complete silence was just over the horizon and he knew it.

The old four-wheeler roared down the long driveway towards the mailbox, at one point hitting a pretty deep rut in the road, making both his and Wife's butts leave the seat for a split second. What Old Man didn't notice was that the doll had fallen from Wife's grasp when they hit the hole. He only realized it when Wife began to stand up, which made him stop a little too quickly. Both of them lost their balance, but just before they tumbled off he was able to hit the kill switch, bringing the machine to a slow halt a few feet ahead of them.

They landed in the road on their backs behind the four-wheeler. Wife was on the right side and he on the left. With his heart in his throat, he jumped up from the hard ground - not so easy for a person of his age -

and hurried over to Wife, who lay flat on the ground, smiling up at him.

"Are you alright?" He asked, kneeling down next to his smiling wife. He put his hand under her back to sit her up, but she shook her head in refusal. Then with one hand, she grabbed a hold of his jacket and attempted to pull him down closer to her, while her other hand patted the gravel beside where she lay.

Confused, he did as instructed, and sat down beside her. She continued to smile and pat the ground until he realized that what she wanted was for him to lie down next to her, which he did. Once he was down, he put his left arm under her head as a pillow, and when he did she moved her head over and onto his chest, nestling him. The next thing he heard was, "Love you."

He laid on the hard, cold ground, holding his wife's body next to his and began to laugh. Then she began to laugh, just as he heard the sound a truck come to a speedy halt on the road behind them, spraying loose gravel as it did.

Old Man heard a door slam shut, and then the sound of footsteps, much huffing and puffing, and then, "Oh my God! Oh My God!"

The runner was standing over them. It was Leroy Graham, their mailman. His face was as white as the curly white hair that stuck out of the sides his red and black checkered hat.

"Hugh, what the hell man? Are you two okay? I mean, when I saw your four-wheeler and then you laying here, I about shit my pants. Do you want me to call for help?"

"No, Leroy, we're okay, but if you could go get the baby in the road, and bring it back to us, I sure would appreciate it", he pointed back behind the wheeler.

"A baby? Oh my God, Hugh, what's going on?" He cried, turning to run as fast as he could up the driveway to where the doll lay in the ditch on its side. Relieved, he walked slowly back to the two bodies cuddling together in the road, laughing. Leroy shook his head, as if trying to regain some sanity. But he handed the doll to them.

All humor aside, Old Man was glad to see the color returning to Leroy's face. He felt bad for the man. He knew he was shook up.

"Are you sure you don't want me to call someone? I mean it's no problem. At least let me help you guys up", Leroy offered.

Right then, the clouds moved over, covering the sun and a light snow began to fall.

"No, we're good, Leroy. Eileen's at the house. Trust me, we're good, right where we are. But if you don't mind, would you do me one last favor, and bring us the mail?"

68

Leroy stood still for a few more seconds. "It's Sunday Hugh, ain't no mail today. I was just on my way over to Evert's to watch a football game, and I just happened to look up your driveway and - hell man, you scared me to death."

From the ground, Old Man offered an apology. "I'm sorry, Leroy. I sure didn't mean to. I appreciate you stopping, I really do. Now you go on and watch that football game, and tell Evert we said hello."

Turning towards his truck, the shaken mailman said, "Okay then. I guess I'll be seeing ya."

It was a few more minutes before Old Man heard Leroy shut the truck door and start the engine. He knew they were being watched, so he stifled his laughter until the man was gone.

After about another ten minutes or so, their laughing evaporated and he sensed that she had left that place of togetherness. He stood her up to dust her off and assess any possible damage. Finding none, he loaded them back on the four-wheeler and headed towards home.

Fun, that's what that was, he thought. Fun, fun, fun. Old Man chuckled thinking about how crazy it must have looked with the two of them laying in the road the way they were. He chuckled even more when he thought of how mail carriers were like barbers; soon everyone in town who knew them, and even those who didn't, would hear of their little episode. But he didn't care, he was so friggin' happy.

BOY

This is the first day I could stand without feeling that stabbing pain, so I decided to test out my landing skills by flying around the fields, landing here and there on fence posts and barren branches.

I flew in and out of the naked trees, testing out my skills, dodging the harassing black giants who scavenge the fields for bits of corn. They were big, and their red eyes threatened me every time I flew past them.

Personally, I don't like corn. I don't know how I know this, but I do. They could have the dry old corn for all I care. What I do know is that the danger I felt around them was familiar. I knew in my gut that they were my enemies and meant harm, just as I knew that I didn't like corn. It's a feeling I'd better pay attention to.

Satisfied, but feeling danger from the black giants, I flew back to the safety of my new winter home. On my way, I saw The Furry One sleeping in the sun near the fence line. I thought, why not? So, I joined her.

She didn't protest in the least when I landed on her back and nestled into her soft fur. We both snoozed in the sun, until a loud growling in my belly woke me up. She must have been hungry too, because when I took off towards my house, she did too.

We made it home just as the sky started to throw small white balls to the ground. My other bird friends ran inside as fast as they could, and The Furry One was right behind them.

I have to admit that I'm thankful for not having to live in the fields, or the trees, not just yet. I'm grateful to the Old Man and Wife for having saved me.

THAT'S IOWA FOR 'YA

The temperature began to drop as the snow fell upon on the farm. This snow wouldn't last. It never did this time of year in Iowa. As they entered the kitchen, Old Man thought back to when they were kids, and how excited they were at the first snow. He remembered how, by the time they gathered up their warm clothes, found their sleds and headed outside, the snow had already begun to melt.

He chuckled, "That's Iowa for 'ya."

The smell of homemade chili and cornbread filled the house and the falling snow made everything inside that much warmer and cozier.

Jacob sat at the table, peeling off his work clothes, while Eileen tugged at one end of his leg, grunting as she tried to remove one muddy boot clinging to his sweaty foot. In between her grunts, she delivered a scolding for not removing his boots at the door.

Old Man winked as he passed his grandson on his way to a chair. Removing the flannel shirt and sweater from Wife's shoulders, he maneuvered around the soiled baby doll in her arms. Then before heading to kitchen to make them something warm to drink, he wiped his wife's runny nose and patted Eileen on the shoulder.

"I was just thinking of sending out a search party to look for you two. Where the heck were you all this time, Hugh?" Eileen asked.

Old Man couldn't help but grin. "I guess I can't keep track of what day it is anymore. I thought it was a mail day, so we went to pick it up. When I figured out that it was Sunday and there was no mail, we farted around at the end of the driveway until it started to snow, it took a little longer than I had expected."

He wanted to add that she was sure to be hearing about it soon enough, but he didn't.

Old Man casually changed the subject, by asking Jacob about his day with the calves. They talked back and forth from the dining room to the kitchen, until Jacob was finally free of his boots and standing right next to his Grandpa, looking up at him.

"They're so great Grandpa and really smart! They already know where their own stalls are. I fed them and started to lead them back to the barn, when they just went right past me, going right into their stalls, like they knew whose was whose. It was awesome."

"That's great son, but do me a favor. Don't trust them quite yet, them calves can be sneaky, believe it or not. They're not as smart as you give them credit for. They just learn early on what's called 'repetition'. It's like follow-the-leader. They're creatures of habit, which means that the more they do something; the more it becomes natural for them, get it?"

"I hear what you are saying Grandpa, but my girls are different!" Jacob said defensively.

On his way back to the table, Old Man put an end to the conversation with his grandson by adding, "Well, who knows, Jacob? Maybe Aunt Fara gave you special ones."

Satisfied, Jacob smiled and nodded in agreement, then headed into his room to change his clothes. Eileen reminded him as he walked away that he had to take a shower, because the following day was a school day. She wasn't positive, but she thought she heard him say, "damn it", as he closed his bedroom door.

Night came fast, and the snow came hard. Everyone devoured the chili and cornbread. Eileen and Jacob headed to their rooms for the night while Old Man sat awhile longer at the table, looking at the woman next to him. Even with her vacant eyes and chili all over her chin, he thought her beautiful. Reaching over he dabbed at her face with a napkin from the pile wedged inside the blue plastic napkin holder. Charly had made it in Boy Scouts when he was seven out of a plastic detergent jug bought from the Fuller Brush Man. This door-to-door salesman was a common visitor back in the days of past, someone you could count on stopping in once a week, kind of like the Jehovah Witnesses, but different.

Charly had drawn around his little hands and fingers with a marker on the plastic jug and, with the help of his dad, cut it to make a napkin holder.

Old Man remembered that project and the day they made it, and was grateful for the memory. He wondered whether Wife, who stared at it could remember what it was, or that it had been a gift to her from her son for Mother's Day, but he doubted it. Now, it was just something to focus on, to get lost in. And although he felt it was unfair, he was beginning to accept, rather than feel sad.

Over the past few weeks, something in him had shifted. It was an awakening, a clarity one might say, replacing the sadness and self-pity that had been smothering him. Old Man was no longer going to waste what precious time he had left on this earth being sad or feeling sorry for himself.

Calling it a night, he lifted Wife and her doll up from the chair and led them into the bedroom. Across the hall was Jacob's room. His door was open and so were his eyes and ears. Before his Grandpa shut his door, Jacob heard him tell his Grandma, "Thanks for a great day, Wife."

The next day, Eileen took Jacob to school and let Old Man know that she planned on visiting her parents, Bob and Katherine, in their new digs before she returned to the farm.

Old Man's routine with Wife would resume for the time being. He watched the snow drip off the roof and decided to keep Wife inside for a while, at least until things dried out some. The dampness was hard on old bones, and after their excursion the day before, he knew she must be a little sore. He certainly was.

Jacob got up early to feed the chickens and let his buddies out to roam the fenced yard before he headed off to school. When Eileen returned, Old Man would double-check on the critters, just to give him something to do. In the meantime, he sat at the table and watched Wife's chest rise and fall as she slept peacefully in her chair.

Sipping the last bit of tea in his cup, he noticed the pad of paper sitting on the other side of the table. It was the Thanksgiving list.

"Wow", he said, as he looked through the names. There were at least three dozen people on that list. Eileen had even included the round bossy one, Eliza, to the list of names and, naturally, next to her name was her husband Charles's, a good man and a hard-working son-of -a gun.

Old Man heard that Charles was now delivering pizzas on the weekends for Bambinos, an Italian restaurant in Ottumwa. What he didn't know, not that it was any of his business, was whether Charles did it because he needed the extra money, or because he needed to get out the house. He thought the latter was probably more like it.

He reviewed the list a little longer, realizing how all of the names before him fit into the puzzle he called his life, and he was truly thankful for each and every one of them - even "bossy pants."

Glancing one more time at the list before setting it back on the table, a light bulb went off, and he immediately knew what his afternoon project would be. With all of these people coming they were going to need tables and benches, so he ripped off a blank sheet of paper from the pad and began sketching. Once the critters were checked on, he would dig into that pile of lumber stacked up in the barn, and maybe even put a fire in the old wood stove so Wife could sit in there while he worked.

Perfect, he thought, just perfect.

BOYS WILL BE BOYS

When Jacob got off the school bus that afternoon, he was mad, storming all the way up the driveway and into the house. He walked through the kitchen door, slamming it behind him and stomping to his room without taking off his coat or boots.

"Hey. Hey, hey, young man", Eileen barked, as she followed him to his room. "Just what the heck has gotten into you?"

Jacob plopped down on the bed and she sat down next to him, prepared to give him a lecture. But before she could, he blurted out, "I got into a fight today. I didn't want to mom, but he stole my damn gloves, and on top of that, Ms. Ashley made ME sit in her office, ME!"

Eileen's face was stricken, both with his news and his favorite swear word, but before she could say anything about either, he went on. "When I went to my locker to get dressed for the bus, my gloves were mysteriously gone! I know it was him, because at recess he told me that he didn't have any gloves. I remember that very well, because he was teaching me some new words right before the bell rang. I was so mad mom. I punched him right in the face!"

"Who is 'him,' honey? Who did you punch in the face?" She asked with urgency.

Jacob looked at his mom and made a snotty face. "Dan. Dan-The-Man, a thief and a big ole bully. Oh, and a liar too. That's what he is."

This was the first time that Eileen had heard of her son having any conflict with anyone. With her guts in a knot, she tried to think of what to say to say to him to calm him down so they could talk about it.

"Nothin' worse than a liar and a thief. That's what you and Grandpa always say, right mom?" Jacob asked defensively.

"Well, yes, that's what we always say Jacob, but we also say that you shouldn't hit anyone. Remember that part?" His mother countered.

"That's not what Grandpa says. He says that you don't hit anyone 'for no good reason,' and I had a good reason!" He protested, his face getting redder and tears rolling down his cheeks.

"For future reference honey, the only time you have my permission to hit someone is if they are hurting you, and there's no other choice. Got it? And as far as this Dan-The-Man stealing your gloves, I'll handle that. I'll talk to Ms. Ashley tomorrow and get this straightened out."

Mary Ashley was Jacobs fifth grade teacher, and Eileen felt certain that she would straighten all of this out, but what bothered her more than him being in trouble at school was the look on her sons face. It pained her that she couldn't shield him from the ugly stuff life throws at a child.

She reached for her son's fisted hand, hoping that this turmoil would be the last. But in her heart, she knew it wouldn't be. Unfortunately, she knew that it was just the beginning of growing up.

"Hey, why don't you head outside and check on your girls? Grandpa's already out there somewhere, maybe you can talk to him about this, but only if you want to, okay bud?" Hugging him, and feeling his return hug lightened the sick feeling in her stomach.

He was almost to the door when Eileen said, "Hey, you didn't tell me what words you learned today."

He turned and answered. "Farming words mom, like 'Corn Hole and Dick Weed.' Dan said that Dick Weed is something that grows all over down south. I'm not sure what Corn Hole means, but I'll ask Grandpa. He'll know, being a farmer an' all."

Then just like that, he was gone.

"Lord!" She said aloud, when a sound like a giggle came from behind her. She quickly turned around and walked over to the little body lying in the big chair. Wife was still asleep, her eyes closed. Eileen wondered, as she looked down at her, if Betty could dream. And if she could, would her dreams be as mixed up as her waking world? She pondered the question as she pulled up the afghan lying at Wife's feet, tucking it tight against her shoulders and neck. With closed eyes, Betty grinned.

Eileen gently touched one side of Betty's face and whispered, "Sleep well you little eavesdropper", before walking into the kitchen to make supper.

By the time Jacob got to the barn, his school turmoil was no longer his major concern. He entered the barn at a trot, shutting the large doors behind him

"Hey Grandpa", he said, walking over to where Old Man was busy measuring boards on a couple of saw horses.

"Hey buddy", his Grandpa answered, not looking up. "Bob and Daisy are out in the East yard where they can stay until we're done here. Come here and hold this board for me while I cut it. This is the last one", he said, wiping the sweat from his brow and glancing down at his grandson.

74

"You're just in time to help me screw all of this together", he pointed to the large pile of lumber stacked up near the old wood stove that was putting off some serious heat.

"Whoa, is it hot in here, or what?" Jacob said, peeling his coat off and flinging it over the side of one of the stalls. "What the heck are you making?"

"What we're making, son, are the tables and benches for our Thanksgiving dinner. Looks like your mom is inviting the whole county out here for dinner, and there sure isn't enough room in the house for all of us. We're going to have a feast out here in the barn. What do you think of them apples?"

"Sounds good to me", Jacob said, when all of a sudden, he noticed above them on one of the large beams, the sign his Grandpa made for him. 'Jacob's Farm' was painted in big black letters, and surrounding that were strategically placed arrowheads, seventy-odd years' worth circling the words. It was beautiful.

"That is so cool Grandpa. Wow, you made that for me? Thanks a lot. That just turned my shitty day into an awesome one!" He said, staring up at the hand-crafted sign, which hung next to a similar, but faded one that read, 'Charly's Farm'.

"Well, I'm glad you like it son, but you got to knock off that language of yours. You're too damn young to be cussing like that, especially around an adult. It's disrespectful." Old Man walked the few feet to his grandson, and put his arms around him. "Hear me boy? Enough of that, okay?"

"Whatever you say, Grandpa. And thanks a ton, I love it "

The two of them spent the rest of the afternoon and early evening screwing together the tables and benches Old Man cut out of scrap lumber. When the last bench was assembled, Old Man set it underneath a table with the others. Then, they stood back and admired their work

"Perfect", Old Man said.

"Yep, perfect", Jacob echoed.

"Now you can go get your calves and put them in for the night. I'll see ya at the house." But before Old Man walked out of the barn, he turned around and said, "Thanks buddy, I couldn't have done it without you."

Jacob winked at his Grandpa, which put another smile on the tired old face.

That evening, as half of the house was already in bed, Eileen decided to call it a night. Before she headed up the stairs, Old Man asked her how the invitations for Thanksgiving were going. There was no light on in the house except for a faint yellow bulb over the stove, but he could see that she looked preoccupied and she was.

Jacobs turmoil was weighing on her, and she had forgotten to ask his Grandpa if Jacob had talked to him about anything. Now she didn't have the energy, so it would have to wait.

Turning around to answer the man standing in the yellow glow, she sighed. "Pretty darn good, so far. Everyone I've called says they're coming. Now all I have to figure out is the menu, and where to get a zillion tables and chairs. Maybe I can borrow some from the church. Don't worry though, I'll figure it out."

"How about you not worrying about that part sweetie? Jacob and I will be in charge of the seating and of getting the barn ready. Trust me, we can handle it", Old Man assured her.

He wanted more than anything to surprise her and to make her happy. They were a team after all, and it was one of the few ways he could show his appreciation for all that she did.

"Wife is going to supervise the project, we've already talked about it", he said with a wink.

That cracked Eileen up, erasing the shadow of worry on her face. "I think I kind of overdid it with the invites, but I didn't want to leave anyone out, if you know what I mean?" She said.

"Sure, I know what you mean, so don't worry about it. We can handle it. You just focus on the food part okay? Now let's get some sleep", he said, vanishing into the darkness of the stairs.

Eileen took the steps up to her room two at a time "I hope I can", she murmured.

SECRETS WE KEEP

Why didn't you or the office call me, Mary?" Eileen asked Jacob's teacher. She was obviously a little irritated, as she stood in the school's main hallway the following morning.

"To be honest with you, Eileen, I forgot all about it", Mary Ashley said. "It was crazy around here yesterday, with everyone getting ready for the big football game last night. Apparently, after last week's home game with Pella, a bunch of kids tore up the high school field. A hundred kids from Des Moines plus their parents were here for the game. It was crazy, so it was all I could do to keep track of our own kids."

"I'm awful sorry", she added.

"This morning, I made sure that Jacob and Dan were separated and, at least for the time being, everything is fine. They're in gym right now, ignoring each other.

"Please", Mary said, motioning to a closed door, "let's go in here and talk."

When they walked into the small office off of the main hallway, the school administrator got right to the point. "Do you know Dan, the boy involved, Eileen? Mary asked.

"No, I don't. I've never heard his name before yesterday", Eileen said. "But whoever he is, Jacob was pretty mad at him when he got home."

"I don't blame him for being mad", Mary agreed. "I was mad too, but not at Dan or Jacob. I was mad at the whole situation. I hate it when kids fight. But, did Dan steal Jacob's gloves? I don't know. He didn't admit to it, and I didn't find them in his locker or in his backpack. Does Dan need gloves? No, he doesn't. I know because I bought him a pair a few weeks ago, and since I didn't find the gloves on him or in his things, I couldn't go any further with Jacob's accusation. Whatever its worth, I'm having Deputy Austen come to school this afternoon, before the bell rings, to talk with Dan; you know, give him a talk about stealing, just in case I'm wrong."

Austen, another lifelong resident of Ottumwa, became a Deputy of Wapello County right out of high school. Eileen knew his parents, and even babysat him a time or two when she was a teenager. Now in his late 20's, single, 6'2" and fit as a fiddle, he looked pretty intimidating, especially in his uniform. That is, until he smiled. When that guy smiled, he became the most beautiful man Eileen had ever seen. Ever. And she wasn't the only one in the county who felt that way. Almost every woman, old or young, unless they were blind, thought the same thing.

Aunt Fara told Eileen once, that after being pulled over by Austen for driving her tractor down the middle of the highway, that he could pull her over every day for the rest of her life and she wouldn't care.

Part of Austen's beauty was his perfect skin color, a bronze and chocolate mix attributed to his bloodline from the Fox and Sauk Indian tribe. He was a descendant of Chief Wapello himself, for whom the county was named. The young county deputy, the great chief's descendant, was graced with the same facial structures that were carved into the eighteen foot tall statue of the Chief that was located in the town of Agency, a few miles out of Ottumwa.

Mary continued, "I'll do my best to keep those boys separated until this blows over, and I promise that if there are any more problems, I'll call you. No one needs this kind of crap, not you, not me, and certainly not Leila. Do you know Leila Morgan, Eileen?" Mary asked.

Eileen couldn't place the name. "I don't think so", she said. "Should I?"

Mary stood up to shut the door to the office before she went on, brushing her short faded blonde hair away, exposing deep worry lines above her almond-shaped eyes. When she sat back down this time, it was on the edge of the chair, closer to Eileen. "She's Dan's mom. She used to be a nurse at Sylvan woods when it first opened. You know that retirement community downtown?"

"Sure, I know it. My mom and dad just moved in there. Where's Leila working now? Maybe I've seen her around."

"I doubt it", Mary said slowly. "She is currently in prison over in Mitchellville."

"In prison? What for?" Eileen gasped.

Mary sighed. "It's a long story, a long sad story. But hopefully, for Dan's sake, one with a good ending. I guess it's no secret, but I'd like it if you kept what I am about to tell you to yourself, okay?"

"Certainly", Eileen said, noticing tears filling Mary's eyes.

Mary forged ahead. "Shortly after her husband, Jud, left for his second tour in Afghanistan, Leila sustained a minor injury and became addicted to pain pills. She started stealing them from work, and by the time Jud returned home, she was jobless, living in Comanche with Dan, and shooting up heroin."

Suddenly, Eileen blurted out, "Jud? Jud Morgan? I went to school with him. He was always such a shy, sweet guy. Where's he now?"

Clearing her throat, Mary spoke, but barely above a whisper. "Jud killed himself a few years ago, right before Leila was sentenced. I guess he couldn't shake the ugliness of his time in Afghanistan, or handle the lack of stability he came home to. I don't really know why he did it. I just know that one day he drove Dan to school, walked him inside, got back in his car, drove down to the river and shot himself in the head. No note, no nothing. He just cracked, like so many that come home from that senseless war."

"Oh, my God, that poor little boy. So, who's been taking care of him?" Eileen asked.

Mary wiped away her tears, saying, "I have. Leila is my little sister. I promised her I would take care of Dan until she got out of prison, and I have. Actually, I was taking care of him before that. Things were so messed up, ya know? My sister is a good person, Eileen, a really good person. She just got sucked into la-la land, where you don't have to deal with anything, or feel anything, and the price she paid was huge. Drugs don't discriminate between the good and the bad. They take anybody to

78

hell and back, Back only if they're lucky.

Anyway, she gets released next week", Mary concluded, with a large sigh.

"I can't tell by the look on your face if that's a good thing, Mary, or a bad thing", Eileen said, leaning forward.

"Oh, it's a good thing alright, a very good thing. We have been waiting a long time for this day to come. Dan and I have been driving over to Mitchellville every other week for two years, just so they could stay connected. I didn't want either of them to lose faith. I believe that where there is faith there is hope. That little boy needs his mom and my sister needs her son", she said, brightening.

"Leila's been doing so well. She's ready to move on with her life. She even finished her Master's degree while she was in there. I forget in what; something to do with psychology, I think", she said, her voice trailing off and her attention now lost in the patterns on the tile floor of the office.

It was obvious to Eileen that there was something bothering Mary. She thought that there was much more to the story. Mary's sudden silence was torture. It was like reading a story and finding out, part of the way through it, that the rest of the pages were missing.

Eileen broke the spell. "Mary, is there another problem?"

Shaking her head up and down, almost violently, Mary said, "Yes, there's a problem, two in fact. One is that my sister is going to be sent away, yet again, on the day after Thanksgiving. Her release stipulates that she move into a woman's halfway house in Minnesota for eight months. She just told me that yesterday."

"Dan doesn't know this yet. How do you tell a little boy that his mom is going away from him again without that affecting him negatively? I'm so afraid that this will undo everything we've worked for over the past two years."

"Oh Mary, I'm so sorry" Eileen cried, but before she could say more, Mary held up her hand.

"The second, and most concerning, problem I have right now, is that I just found out that I have breast cancer, which means I also have to go away, at least until spring. I can't take Dan with me while I have surgery, and I'll be no good to him during the months of treatment. So, I'm worried sick. There is no more family, just me. I honestly don't know what to do." Finished at last, Mary looked at Eileen through tears.

That was it. Both women started crying hard. They clutched each other, as if to keep from falling off of their chairs. And when the crying faded, hiccups took over,

Remembering where she was and who she was, Mary stood up, wiped her face with the back of her hand, and straightened her blouse and slacks. She was clearly embarrassed that she allowed the dam to break, in front of the parent of one of her students.

Without looking at Eileen, she apologized for having poured out her personal life. "I went too far. I wasn't thinking. Once I started talking, it just all came out. I'm sorry", she said. Forgive me."

Eileen knew that she couldn't just walk away and go about her life, as if she knew nothing of these people. "I have an idea", Eileen said, as she stood up and squeezed Mary's shoulders, mangling the blouse that had just been straightened. "Whatever you do, Mary, don't lose hope. You said it yourself, there's always hope."

Eileen started for the door, then turned back around, "I'll contact you in the next couple days. You just keep those two boys in line. Oh, and don't forget about coming out for Thanksgiving. The boys will just have to put their issues aside. There'll be no fighting on that day. I'll make sure of it, okay?"

She waited for Mary's nod, and when it came, she opened the door and walked away.

Outside the school, Eileen sat in her car for a few minutes to pull her wits together, then called Old Man on her cell phone.

TAKING CARE OF THEIR OWN

Hugh was giddy when he answered the phone. Eileen could tell by his voice, and the way he dove right into telling her about a big surprise that he was in high spirits. But she cut him off.

"Sorry to interrupt, Hugh, but I'm in kind of a hurry. I was just checking in to see if you guys are okay. I was hoping to stop at Sarah's house before I came home. Is that alright? I'd say that I'll be about another hour or so?."

"Sure, honey, we're fine", Hugh said. "My 'supervisor' and I just finished up a project in the barn, and thought we'd come in for some lunch. Good timing, eh? You go on and tell Sarah we said hello."

"Will do, Hugh. Thanks. I'll see ya soon", she said, hanging up.

Eileen turned off the highway and onto the county road leading to Sarah's house. A large sign, reading "Sarah's Stables" stood along the side of the road. In case anyone missed the sign, they wouldn't miss the huge arrow a little farther down the driveway that pointed first time visitors in the right direction.

She was betting on Sarah being home. She knew she gave riding lessons in the afternoons, and hoped that it was early enough to get there before the lessons started.

Sarah's driveway was long, typical of old Iowa farmsteads. On each side of the driveway stood huge old oak trees, protecting the ones who traveled there. Those trees were planted long before either she, or Sarah, or even their parents were born.

None of Sarah's family wanted to take over the farm after her Grandparents passed away. All of her siblings moved away right after high school, and her parents retired to Florida shortly after that. They hadn't understood why their daughter, a young single woman, would choose to live in 'that old house'.

They tried, to no avail, to encourage Sarah to at least move to Des Moines, where there were more opportunities for someone her age. But Sarah had no desire to flee rural life and, unlike her family, she loved the old farmhouse. Built in the mid-1800's by her grandfathers' father, that history alone made it special to her. Except for the lack of insulation, it was perfect.

Over the years, Sarah had the old barn torn down, replacing it with a new, larger, heated one. It housed eight of her horses and six boarders. The barn and tack rooms were packed with saddles and other essential gear, but the part Sarah was most proud of was the spacious and popular riding arena in the center of the barn.

She always had a few rescue dogs around the farm, but horses were her life and her love. She made her living by giving riding lessons, boarding horses, and breeding horses. Breeding was where her meat and potatoes came from, and though she was just squeaking by, she was comfortable.

Eileen thought of how inviting the old place looked, as she parked her car in front of the long, covered porch, generously decorated with pumpkins, gourds and stalks of corn. Eileen wanted the same warm effect for the Thanksgiving festivities in their barn.

Rocking chairs sat here and there along the porch, with all but one being vacant.

A woman in a red hat, with a pipe hanging from her thin lips, rocked back and forth, waving at the visitor. Eileen smiled and waved back. This was Aunt Fara.

Good she thought, "Now I can kill two birds with one stone."

The front door flew open, and two huge Rottweilers came out, wagging their tails as they ran to greet her. In their wake came Sarah, dressed in her usual attire of blue jeans, buffalo plaid flannel shirt, and worn riding boots. A long brown braid, tangled in copper highlights, reminded Eileen of a horse's mane as it hung to one side of the woman's head.

"Hey girl!" Sarah said, as she stepped out onto her porch, and took a seat in a nearby rocker. "I was going to call you tonight to thank you for the Thanksgiving invite. Sounds like a great plan, so count me in. We were just talking about what we should bring. I'm not much of a cook, but I make a mean pecan pie. Any more suggestions?"

"Pie is great. Make seven or eight of them", Eileen said, chuckling. "I should probably be keeping track of what people tell me they're bringing. It's getting confusing. I know Evert said he'd be bringing hams, and Mike's smoking up about ten turkeys. That should cover the meat. Oh, and Pastor Dale said he was going to fry up a ton of chicken livers. That man sure has a thing for chicken livers."

"Yum", Fara said, letting a cloud of smoke escape her mouth. There was a hint of apple, and possibly citrus, to the tobacco. The aroma was as inviting as the porch was festive.

"It's going to end up being one big-ass smörgåsbord", Eileen said. So, bring whatever you want. How's that sound, for taking me off the hook?"

Then, eager to get on with the real reason for her visit, she changed the subject. "Hey, Aunt Fara, I'm glad you're here. I have something I want to ask you, actually, both of you."

Fara reached down and picked a handful of walnuts out of the basket sitting next to her rocker. "Shoot", she said, then began shucking one of the oily black balls, exposing the rich nut inside "I don't hear so good these days, sugar, so come on over here and tell me what's on your mind."

"Yes'm", Eileen said, choosing a chair between the two women. Before Eileen had the chance to begin, Fara asked, not looking up from her walnut shucking. "How's things over at the Roberts? Hugh and Betty okay?"

She had been at the pharmacy that morning and got an earful from Tom, the pharmacist, about Leroy's experience the Sunday before when he found Hugh and Betty lying in the road, giggling.

"Actually, things are great, Fara. Hugh's acting like a man on a mission now that Jacob's around, and Jacob hasn't quit glowing since we moved out there, thanks in part to you. Hugh loves those calves something awful and, well, there's a light in his eyes that wasn't there before, ya know? I don't know if it's because of Jacob, or because of the animals. All I know is that Old Man doesn't seem as sad as before."

Eileen thought about mentioning the bird, Boy, but decided against it. That was too long a story, and she wanted to get to the big reason she came. "All I know is that some thing's different, and in a good way."

"That's great to hear", Sarah said, before Fara had the chance.

"Do either of you know Leila Morgan?" Eileen suddenly asked.

"Of course I do", Fara said. "Known her since she was born, like you girls. Her grandmother and me were pals, back in the day. Had a lot of fun too. Why do you ask?"

Eileen smiled. "Who the heck don't you know, Fara?"

"Well, I don't know the President of the United States!" They all cracked up at that remark.

When laughing died down, Eileen got serious again. "Well, the thing is, I just came from Jacob's school where I was having a meeting with Mary Ashley about some trouble between Jacob and a boy named Dan."

Fara asked, "You mean Dan The Man, or some other Dan?"

Astonished, Eileen answered, "Oh, I mean Dan The Man alright, but how I may ask do you know that he calls himself that?"

The weathered boards under Fara's rocker creaked as she leaned forward wearing a smug look. "Cause I gave him that name, that's how!

"Of course you did", she laughed, then turned to Sarah.

"I suppose you know Dan The Man too?"

"Sure do", Sarah said. "I've been giving him riding lessons every other Saturday for about a year now, right Fara?"

Fara nodded, "That's right."

It was no secret that Fara paid for just about anything children wanted to learn, particularly if their parents couldn't afford it. It didn't matter what kind of lessons they were; piano, swimming, dance, whatever. It just hadn't occurred to Eileen before that riding lessons were a part of that.

"Go on now", Fara said, taking a long draw from her pipe.

"So, you know about Leila being in prison and that her husband killed himself?" Eileen ventured.

Both women looked at each other, nodding in unison.

"Well, how come I didn't know anything about it then?" She said. It bothered her that she didn't know this boy, or his mom, or about poor Jud, when apparently it was common knowledge.

"Sad story, but not all sad stories have sad endings", Fara said.

"Mary's been doing a damn good job with that boy, though, and his mama's going to be getting out real soon. They'll be all right. Now let's hear your question."

"Finally", Eileen said, albeit a bit too loud.

"Since you two seem to know most all of what I was going to say, I'm guessing you know the rest of the story too, eh?"

Fara said, "Try me."

"Mary told me not thirty minutes ago that, yes Leila is getting out next week, but that she's being sent away right after Thanksgiving to some halfway house in Minnesota. She'll be gone for another eight months."

Fara's eyebrows raised, confirming that she didn't know the rest of the story. It was Eileen that wore a smug look on her face now.

Being a beat ahead of Fara was a first, and probably a last, so she kept going. "Mary also shared with me that she has breast cancer and is scheduled to have surgery in Des Moines soon. She plans on staying there for her treatment because it makes sense."

Again, Fara interrupted.

"Shit!" Then, "Dammit!" She spat out, while throwing a walnut into the yard. "Just when those poor folks could see the light at the end of the tunnel, the devil himself turns the light off! Now what's going to happen, did she say?"

"That's why I'm here." Eileen continued. "I was kind of hoping that Sarah would consider taking the boy in until either his mom or his Aunt comes home."

Sarah couldn't hide the effect Eileen's words created. The look on her face was sheer horror.

"What, me? I don't like kids! You know I don't like kids!"

Both Fara and Eileen smothered a laugh. They knew Sarah preferred animals to most people-everyone knew that-but they also knew that most of her clients were children, so 'hating' them was simply not true. She was great with kids.

Sarah stood up and began pacing the length of the creaky porch. "Tell her Aunt Fara, tell her how I don't like kids. What the heck would I do with a kid anyway? Hell, I'd probably lose him somewhere, or forget to feed him and he'd starve to death, or something. I can't take in a kid", she mumbled, walking back and forth and then standing in front of Eileen. "I'm not the right person for that job, Eileen, I swear it. An hour or so a day is just about as long as I can handle a kid. To be honest, the idea scares me to death, What about you? You already have one, what's one more, huh?"

Fara and Eileen were still laughing, not really at Sarah, but at how she instantly came unglued at the mere idea of having to take care of a child. It was funny, for sure.

"All I know is that we have to do something", Eileen said. "We can't let that boy go to foster care to live with strangers. Remember, Sarah, I don't even know who this boy is, so that makes me a stranger. Besides, you both seem to know Dan The Man pretty well."

Fara stood up slowly, indicating that she was done with the porch and the dilemma presented on it. It took her a minute to straighten her body after sitting for a while. Once she was upright she said, "We are going to do something. And no, we are definitely not going to let him go live with strangers."

She stuck her pipe in her mouth and lit it again. "I have to think about this", she said. Then, without another word, she stepped off the porch and walked over to her truck, crawled inside and drove away.

"She's the boss", Sarah said, watching the old pickup bounce down the driveway, the red hat behind the wheel inside disappearing through the tunnel of oaks.

"Yep, she's the boss", Eileen agreed, stepping down from the porch herself. When she reached her car she said, without turning around, "Thanks, Sarah. It was fun scaring the hell out of you - well worth the trip out here."

Eileen thought she heard Sarah mumble something better not heard as the door to the house slammed shut.

DAN THE MAN AND JACOB

By the time Eileen got back to the Roberts' farm, a sheriff's cruiser had parked up next to the kitchen door. She panicked. School wasn't out, she'd just left there an hour before. She prayed that nothing more had happened with the boys. Or worse. Did Wife wander off? Did Old Man have as stroke? Who could've called 911 if he-Hugh was the one down? She shouldn't have left for so long, she thought. What about her parents? They were fine that morning. If there'd been time she'd have puked right there in the car, but there wasn't, so she hopped out of it and ran.

She would've laid rubber all the way to the house, had she had tires on her feet instead of shoes. Hanging onto the counter that divided the kitchen from the dining and living room she took in the people sitting around the table and asked breathlessly, "What the hell's going on here?"

Jacob, quick on the draw, said, "You shouldn't swear in front of children, mom",

A muffled laugh came from the boy sitting next to him. He had dimples, a thick tow head of hair and beautiful teeth, even though one front tooth was missing. She guessed that this was Dan The Man.

"Quiet boy", Old Man said, smacking the top of his grandson's head ever so lightly. "Don't you ever tell your mother what she's supposed to do, 'ya hear me?"

A deflated, "Yes sir", came from Jacob, his obvious attempt to impress Dan The Man appearing to backfire.

"Every thing's all right honey. We're just having a nice talk with the boys. Have a seat." Old Man was trying to calm the situation, but failing.

Still all worked up, Eileen said, "If you don't mind, I'll stand." Then Deputy Sheriff Austen stood up, faced Eileen and smiled. Suddenly, the only thing she could think about was how Fara was missing out. Neither of them wanted to land the deputy for their own. They just enjoyed looking at him. No crime in looking, she thought, as he started to explain why he was there.

"Eileen, I brought the boys out here in the hope that we could clear some things up. I thought it was better to have this conversation here than at school. Isn't that right boys?" He looked sternly at the two wide-eyed boys at the table.

"Yes, sir, that's right", Dan The Man said, standing up from the table as if on cue, then looked down at the table.

Right in the middle of it were Jacob's gloves.

The boy turned to Eileen. "Mrs. Roberts, I did take - I mean, I stole, - Jacob's gloves. It was stupid and I'm sorry I did it. Grandpa Hugh said that as punishment I could work around the farm, if that's okay with you?"

"Grandpa Hugh?" She repeated, glancing over at Old Man, who quickly looked away. Apparently, he had handled the situation in her absence.

Eileen didn't answer the kid right away; she wasn't sure where this was going. Instead she looked over at her son and said, "I want to know what you have to say about this, Jacob."

"Well, mom, in front of these two witnesses", Jacob said, pointing to his Grandpa and the deputy, I told Dan what you told me about stealing, and how you don't never have to steal unless you're hungry, and I mean real hungry, right? And even then, it's still stealing, but God will forgive you for it because you're starving to death. But not if you're starving to death because you're a lazy bum! I also told him how there's no lower life form than a thief and a liar." Jacob smiled, proud of himself.

Eileen couldn't help but grin. "That's not exactly how I said it, honey, but I'm glad you shared it with him anyway. Do you forgive him, Jacob? Do you think he should be punished for taking your gloves?"

Jacob answered right off. "I think when the deputy came into our classroom and took him away was punishment enough, right Dan?"

86

Everyone looked over to Dan, who was nodding his head up and down.

"That was pretty embarrassing", Dan said.

"The rest was kind of cool, mom. Riding out here in a real cop car. I got to sit in the front and 'the fugitive' had to sit in the back."

Jacob laughed and so did 'the fugitive'.

"But do you forgive him?" His mother insisted.

"Yes", Jacob said, "I do."

"Okay then, no more fighting, no more stealing and, furthermore", she said looking right at Dan The Man, "no more teaching Jacob 'farm words'." The last bit nearly made her smile, but she repressed it.

"Do you hear me, Dan?" Eileen asked the boy, whose dimples now vanished as he nodded his head up and down. "Yes'm, I promise", he said.

"Then why don't you boys go on outside and let the grownups talk for a while", she suggested.

Not needing to be told twice, the two boys jumped at the chance and quickly disappeared through the kitchen door, slamming it behind them with a bang.

Then, a small sound came from the Wife's chair. The boys' noisy departure woke her. Now wide awake, her eyes searched the room until landing on Deputy Austen. When the watery blue eyes locked onto his, he nodded and politely greeted her, "How you doin' Mrs. Roberts?"

"Chief", she said, in greeting, nodding back.

There was no mistaking what she said, and Eileen and Old Man looked at each other with discomfort, confirming that they had both heard the same thing.

Old Man quietly got out of his seat to attend to her.

"Time for a potty break", he said, guiding her away from the chair and into the bathroom, not offering Eileen any assistance in the awkwardness that followed the embarrassing remark.

Eileen didn't know what to say. She was surprised that Wife had responded to Austen at all, but shocked by the racial slur coming from the old woman's lips.

Feeling the need to explain dementia and the components of Betty's disease, she began babbling about how 'off the wall' comments are symptoms of brain deterioration.

But, before she got very far, Austen smiled and pointed to the sleeve of his uniform, where in big red embroidery it read, 'Chief'. "Don't sweat it Mrs. Roberts, it's my nickname."

"Thank God", Eileen said, and thought of Fara. She couldn't help but wonder if the old girl had given him his nickname too.

"Being Indian is something I've always been proud of, so when the department said we could add a nickname to our sleeve, I thought, 'hell yah'!" Laughing, he went on, "The Chief Deputy wasn't very happy about there being two 'Chiefs' in the department and suggested I pick a different name. But I played the 'Indian card,' and boom!"

Pointing to his sleeve again, he said, "The rest in history."

Feeling relieved, Eileen sat down in one of the chairs at the table and motioned for Austen to do the same.

"What about the boys? Do you think this is the end of the fighting?" Eileen asked.

"Hard to know for sure", Austen said. "But I can tell you they were both pretty scared when I showed up at school today, which is a good thing. It's a knack I have, scaring the hell out of kids. Of course, the uniform and gun on my hip help some. Once we got into my car to head out here, they seemed to forget they were enemies. The goof-balls even asked me if I'd take the long way, which I did! Hey, want me to give Dan a ride home?"

"No, I think I'll let them hang out for a while. I can drive him home later. I assume Mary knows he's out here?"

"She sure does, but I'll give her a call to let her know you'll be bringing him home later."

"Thank you" Eileen said.

"You know, Mary's pretty strict with that boy", Austen said, as he put on his jacket. "I think kids lie sometimes because the punishment they receive for telling the truth is too severe. It doesn't make it okay to lie, but you know what I mean.'

"Yeah, I guess I do", Eileen said, remembering a time when she had lied to her dad because she was too afraid to tell him the truth. When he found out later that she had lied, he held it against her for a very long time. Too long, she felt. Such a fine line one walks when disciplining a child with fear. Yep, she did know what he meant.

"So, Austen, have you decided what you're going to do for Thanksgiving"? she asked.

"Thanks for reminding me. I was going to talk to you about that when I got out here, but I forgot. Mom and Dad decided to go to Kansas to spend Thanksgiving with my sisters this year, so I'm free! Count me in. Hey, any chance that you invited Sarah?"

"Well, as a matter of fact I did invite Sarah", Eileen answered with a sly smile. "Why do you ask, hmmm? You have 'thing' for her?"

"Well, I don't know if I'd call it a 'thing'. She's been giving me riding

88

lessons the past few weeks and, ahhh, okay I have a 'thing' for her", he said, then blinded her with another gorgeous smile.

"That's great!" She said.

"Now don't you go trying to fix me up. Aunt Fara's already putting her nose in where it don't belong. I've got this, okay?" Then on his way to the door, he asked, "What would you like me to bring? I hear there's a gob of people coming."

"I think you should call Sarah and ask her what she thinks you should bring", Eileen shot back, grinning.

"Women!" He said, walking out into what was left of the afternoon.

Outside, Dan and Jacob were busy playing tag with the little calves, Bob and Daisy. It was Dan's turn to take a break, so he climbed up on one of the boards circling the pen to catch his breath, when he noticed a white picket fence on a hilltop across the field.

"Hey Jacob, what's that over there?" Dan asked, pointing out over the partially snow covered field.

Running hard, and with Daisy right behind him, Jacob reached up with both hands to grab hold of the boards, and climbed up next to Dan. Bob was already on the other side of the pen taking advantage of the lack of competition at the feeding trough.

Jacob cranked his head around to where Dan was pointing, then jumped down on the outside of the fence

"It's a graveyard. Wanna meet my family?" He asked, in all serious-ness.

"Creepy", Dan said, jumping down to catch up. "Why is your family buried out here and not in a real graveyard?"

"This is a real graveyard, it's our graveyard, Jacob replied. Ain't no strangers buried in there, just our family and some cats and dogs, and, I think, my dad's bull is there too. Grandpa says it's important to keep your people close to you. That way, if you need to talk to them, you can just walk out there and sit down for a talk", he said all of this noncha-lantly, kicking snow up into the air with his boot as they walked, and explaining to his new friend how he occasionally comes out there just to be alone. Other times just to talk.

"Creepy", Dan said again.

When they got to the graveyard, Jacob followed the fresh deer tracks over the little white fence, ignoring the open gate on the other side. He motioned for Dan to follow him, as he weaved in and out of the old headstones, stopping when he came upon a newer larger one. Pointing, Jacob said, "Dan, meet Charles James Roberts. My dad."

Dan looked down at the stone and then back over to Jacob. "Died in

2006? That's the year I was born, man."

"See the date? "Jacob said. "That's the day I was born. He died the same day I was born. Never even got to meet him."

Dan felt something he hadn't felt before. Creepy or not, he realized that the dead had just connected him to the boy standing next to him, the same boy he'd bullied and stolen from. Unconsciously, he moved closer to Jacob, and put his arm around his shoulder. Neither said anything until, out of nowhere, came Boy. The bird landed on Jacob's shoulder, right on top of Dan's fingers.

Dan let out a high-pitched scream and tried to shoo the bird away, which tickled Jacob. But the bird didn't leave. Instead, it hovered just above them, until Dan backed away. Then Boy landed once again on Jacob's shoulder.

"Hey Boy, I've been wondering where the heck you were", he said, looking at the bird who looked right back at him.

"You're kidding me, right?" Dan said, putting his hands on top of his head to prevent an unwanted landing or poop bomb.

"Kidding about what? Boy? No, I'm not kidding, he lives here. He lives with the chickens and our cat, Mrs. Nickels. My Grandma saved him after he dive bombed a window, and now he's part of the family. What's the big deal?"

"But you're talking to-to a bird. That's creepy, man!"

Jacob shook his head. "You must like that word, dude, cause you've said it like three times already! And there's nothing creepy about it. I talk to all of the animals, all of the time. What would be creepy is if they talked back to me. But don't worry. So far that hasn't happened", he said as he sat down on the damp ground in front of his dad's grave.

Dan kept an eye on the bird, as he took a seat next to Jacob. Then, both boys studied the headstone, each with his own thoughts.

Dan spoke first. "My dad died when I was six. He killed himself."

Jacob jerked his head around to look at Dan.

"Every Memorial Day, my Aunt Mary takes me to the graveyard in Comanche where he's buried. She pulls weeds and plants flowers around his grave all day. Sometimes, we have a picnic, but usually I just spend the day walking around reading the names on the headstones. I try to memorize as many of the soldiers as I can, so when I go back the next time I can test myself. You know, see if I can find them again. Its huge, that place, with hundreds of soldiers from all different wars buried in there, alongside their families. I've made a game out of finding them. My dad was a soldier and.. "

Dan's voice trailed off.

Lost in his thoughts and appearing to be talking to the wind, the story just faded away. Jacob thought about how envious he was that Dan had known his father. He had known what he looked like, smelled and sounded like. But his envy soon turned to empathy, because, unlike him, Dan truly knew what he was missing. Right then, Boy left Jacob's shoulder and few over to Dan's, as if reading his mind. So, okay, maybe that was a little creepy. Dan's trance ended when Boy landed on one of the arms he had tucked in front him, but this time he didn't scream, or squirm, or try to shoo the bird away. He just turned his head back around to face Charles James Roberts.

"What do ya say to your dad when you're out here?" He asked Jacob.

"Not much, really. Sometimes I tell him about what's going on at school." But lately I've been telling him about the calves, Bob and Daisy. Hey, if I tell you something will you promise not to tell anybody?"

Dan nodded, 'yes'.

"Most of the time when I come out here, it's to cry."

He waited for Dan to laugh, and when that didn't happen, he went on.

"I don't cry because my dad's out here and not in the house. My mom says it's selfish to cry about that when so many kids don't have no family at all. She says I'm lucky because so many people love me. So, I guess I cry because I can't help it. Sometimes, I'm just sad for no reason. Do you ever feel that way?"

Again, Dan nodded, 'yes'.

"How about you? You ever talk to your dad?"

"No", Dan answered, thinking about it hard. "I don't know what I'd say to him. 'I miss you. Why did you go away from me? How's the weather down there?' All the things your mom probably thinks are stupid", he said.

Jacob shook his head. "My mom wouldn't think any of that's stupid. You knew your dad Dan, I didn't. You have a right to miss him and maybe even be mad at him for what he did, but then you need to forgive him, so you can be better. Mom says forgiveness is the key to everything in this world. That's why I forgave you for stealing my gloves", he went on, never taking his eyes off his new friend. "Cancer killed my dad and because of that, I used to be pissed off at God, but I'm not anymore."

"How come?" Dan asked.

"It's that forgiveness thing. I have to believe God has a plan for me. It doesn't mean that the plan is always going to make me happy, but believing it, makes things better. I guess that's what ya call faith, dude. Grandpa says that when someone is in your life, it's because God lent them to you for a while. He says they are a gift, no matter how long they're with us and that we should be grateful, no matter what. What do you think?"

Dan furrowed his brow. "I don't know what I think. My Aunt Mary's a Christian, for sure, and probably thinks about things the same way your Grandpa does. We go to the Baptist church downtown. She says that's what I am, a Baptist, but I don't even know what that means", he said, shrugging his shoulders. "Most people in our church are black. My Aunt says black people don't judge a person the same way white people do, and I think she's right, 'cause I remember when we used to go to a different church where everybody was white and they weren't very friendly. They stared at us a lot. My Aunt said they treated us like we were bugs. Next thing I know, boom! We're Baptists and singin' with the black folk.

The boys sat in silence for a minute before Dan spoke again. "My favorite part about goin' to church, besides not being treated like a bug, is the music. It's awesome. Sometimes I swear the walls are going to come down, the way it rocks in there! When everyone is singin' and swayin' to the music is when I feel God the most. It's powerful, man. Want to go with me sometime?"

"Sounds good to me", Jacob answered. "The only music we have at my church is when Mrs. Johnson plays the organ, and it's not something anyone would want to dance to, that's for sure. How about your mom? Is she a Baptist too?"

"No", Dan said. "My mom doesn't go to church, and when I ask her about it, she says that if there is a God, He knows you love Him no matter where you are or what you call yourself. But my Aunt makes me go, no matter what my mom says. I think, she thinks mom's an atheist."

"What's an atheist?" Jacob asked.

"A person who doesn't believe in God" Dan answered.

"Hmmm, I wonder who she talks to when she's sad or lonely?"

"Don't know, I'll have to ask her that."

"What about your dad?" Jacob asked. "Was he an atheist too?"

"I don't think so, 'cause I remember one time when we were walkin' and found a dead bird in the road. It was Blue Jay. My dad picked it up and spread it's feathers out, like a fan. He said, 'Look at these feathers, son. Look at how perfect each one of these polka dots are on them.' I didn't know Blue Jays had polka dots, but they do. Anyway, then he asked me 'Now, you tell me who else but God could've created something so beautifully perfect?' So, yeah, I'd say dad believed in God."

"Do you live with your Aunt because your mom's an atheist?" Jacob asked then.

"Hardly", Dan laughed. "I thought everybody knew why I lived with my Aunt."

Jacob shook his head 'no' that he didn't know.

"Right after my dad died - killed himself, my mom got sent to Mitchellville, a prison for women, because of something she did with pills. We don't talk about it much, except when we talk about drugs and how they'll mess up your life, like they did mom's. Me and Aunt Mary go visit her a lot. She's doing real good now and", he said, holding up crossed fingers in front of him, "She's coming home next week! Just in time for Thanksgiving. I can't wait!"

"Holy crap, man!" Jacob said, feeling like he had just read a couple chapters from a true crime story. "I guess my mom is right about not feeling sorry for myself. I am lucky! But you're lucky too, Dan. You have your Aunt Mary, your mom, and the Baptists, oh, and me too now!" Jacob added, meaning every word.

Jacob watched Dan digest that, then watched Dan's free hand come up out of his lap to stroke the small feathers on Boy's head.

"If it's okay with you, Jacob, I'd like to come out here again sometime and tell you more about my dad, is that okay?"

"You bet, I'd like to know more about him, and your mom too", Jacob said, then put a hand on his belly and rubbed it around in a circle. "But all that true-life stuff made me hungry. Let's go to the house and get something to eat."

"Sounds good", Dan agreed.

The boys stood up to begin their walk back through the field, but not before bidding a farewell to the cold stone below them. "See ya later, Dad", Jacob called over his shoulder.

"Yeah, nice to meet ya,' Mr. Roberts", Dan said.

Boy simply flew off.

Later that day, when Dan got out of the Roberts' car at his house, he thanked Eileen for letting him come over, not mentioning the fact that Deputy Austen brought him there or why. That was water under the bridge. Before turning to greet his Aunt Mary, Dan said to Jacob "Thanks dude" adding two thumbs up.

As they were backing up to turn around, Eileen gave Mary a thumbs-up as well, and at the same time saw Jacobs mouth dropped open when he realized that Dan's Aunt Mary was his teacher, Ms. Ashley.

Eileen saw the look on Jacob's face. "Small world, isn't it son?"

"Wow, it sure is, mom."

"And it only gets smaller, honey", she said as they drove down the block and turned off onto the highway.

By the time they got back to the farm, the sun was gone from the sky. They hadn't talked much on the drive home, just idle chit chat and not much of that.

Jacob was eager to get home to his critters, and she had decided earlier, having watched the boys laugh and talk while inhaling the peanut butter sandwiches she'd made them, to leave the subject of the day alone. All she could do now was hope they'd both learned a lesson. She had no idea of the depths of what they learned that day, and it hadn't come from the law or the school but from somewhere deep inside two ten-year-old hearts.

She entered the warm house, thinking about what to make for supper. She was banking on something quick, because she still had so much to do to make sure her Thanksgiving plans were on track. Everyone she had asked was coming, and with only one week to go, she was happy to have the number confirmed. But the size of it was also stressing her out.

Old Man had assured her that the tables and chairs were taken care of, an important detail that she hoped was really set, otherwise it would be a disaster. She needed to confirm that with him in a way that wouldn't be insulting or hurtful. He had seemed so excited to be doing his part that she would tread lightly, so as to not take that feeling away from him.

Deciding that everyone would bring something with them, rather than have a set menu, was the best idea she'd had so far. It meant she no longer had to worry about the food, just the seating and decorating the barn.

The house seemed too quiet when she entered. There was no sign of Hugh or Betty. Even after calling their names from the kitchen, only silence greeted her. The doll lay on the floor by the chair. That worried her more than anything, but before she could turn around to go back outside to find them, in they walked, arm in arm.

"Hey you", he said, removing Wife's coat and hanging it up in the closet by the door. "How'd it go?"

"It went fine. The boys seemed okay, even called each other 'dude' a few times and hand bumped like this", she said, taking his free hand and curling it into a fist so she could bump it. "I guess it's something young people do when things are cool between them. I don't really understand it, but it's a good sign. One less thing to worry about", she said, turning to look in the refrigerator.

Now that she didn't have to worry about Hugh and Betty either, she could start making supper. "What were you guys up to?" She asked.

"We were out in the barn settin' up the tables. Wanted to make sure there were enough, 'ya know?" Old Man said, leading Wife to the table.

"You got tables and chairs already?" Eileen asked, relieved and surprised.

"Told you we'd handle it, and we did, didn't we, Wife?"

There was no response to his question as he sat her down.

"We have plenty of seats, and plenty of tables too", he said proudly, not offering any information on how he'd come by them.

"And that old stove heats the barn up pretty darn good. It should be real toasty on Thanksgiving. Want any help with supper?" He asked, walking back into the kitchen.

"No thanks", Eileen said, but if it's okay with you, I think we'll just have soup and sandwiches tonight. Just so all that will be left to do for Thanksgiving is to eat, I'd kind of like to get going on figuring out the decorations."

They smiled at each other, then he said, "You don't have to worry about that either. Got that handled too."

"Got what handled?" She asked, shutting the refrigerator door. Her smile was replaced with evident disappointment. Decorating was the one thing she was really looking forward to doing. It was the fun part.

Seeing the look on her face, Hugh said, "I called 'snoopy pants' today, took all I had in me to do it, but I did it. I remember what a good job she did in the barn for your wedding, so I figured she'd understand when I ask her for any of their leftover pumpkins, and whatever field corn they had, and you know what? She was ecstatic that I asked her. I guess I don't give that woman enough credit."

"Anyway, I figured you might want those things for the tables. She even said she'd come out and help if you wanted her to, and maybe bring Patty with her. Did I do right, honey?"

Relieved, Eileen answered, "That's exactly what I was thinking of doing. Thank you, thank you, thank you!"

Her reaction warmed Old Man's heart.

"Do you think you can scavenge up some corn stalks too? I'd love to tie some around the post. And maybe hay bales to for the kids to sit on?"

"Your wish is my command, young lady", he said, bowing grandly. "I was going to save this part as a surprise, but what the hell. Guess what else we're going to have out there?" Old Man asked, somewhat giddy.

"I have no idea", she said. "Go ahead. Spill the beans."

"A band, that's what!" He crowed. "Tom called this morning to ask if they could bring the band with them for Thanksgiving. The only catch is that we have to feed the band too, but I told him the more the merrier, right?"

Tom was a pharmacist in Ottumwa, and his wife managed a feed company. In the old days, before children and careers, they hung out with Charly and Eileen, and even played at their wedding as their gift to them. These days, their bluegrass band performed during summer festivals, and play at a few bars in town just for fun, a reprieve from their otherwise intense lives.

Eileen grabbed Old Man around the waist and held on tight, her head pressed against his large chest. "This is going to be the best Thanksgiving ever!" She said.

"That it will", he said, sharing in her excitement.

Now, all she had to do was call Mary, but not to talk to her about the boys' issues or to resolve the dilemma Mary was facing, but to extend her Thanksgiving invitation to Dan and his mother. She was riding on the faith that Fara had something in the works by way of a solution for them. She certainly didn't have one. So she hoped that when she called with the invitation, Mary wouldn't bring it up.

BOY

What a day. I ate, I flew around for a while, then I came home and slept in the sun with The Furry One. Then I followed the little guys into the field down by the river and hung out with them for a while.

Then it was home to eat some more. Yep, life is pretty darn good.

THE QUESTIONS KIDS ASK

Jacob entered the kitchen whistling. By this time, Old Man and Eileen sat with Wife at the table working on their supper.

"Take your shoes off and come and eat", his mother said.

"Be right there, mom", he answered.

When Jacob sat down, he dove right into his sandwich. Mouth full, he asked no one in particular, "Did you know that Dan The Man doesn't have a dad either?"

"Please don't talk with food in your mouth, it's gross", his mother said, rather than answering his question.

Old Man and Eileen did know that Dan's father had died, killed himself, but they never discussed it. Eileen had just heard it for the first time a couple days before.

It was Old Man who answered him. "Yes, I knew that son. I remember when it happened. It was a terrible thing for sure, a sad time for many people, especially for his son. Dans daddy's head was never right after being in the war. He just couldn't get back to livin' after he came home. It's a sickness that some veterans have. I think it's called PTSD."

Jacob quit chewing and listened intently to his Grandpa. He always said he couldn't hear when he chewed.

He asked, "Do you think God forgives a person for killing themselves Grandpa?"

"Sure I do", Old Man said. "That's what God does, forgives. It's too bad people don't do the same", he mumbled, not mentioning how he believed that they might not get through the gates of heaven."

Eileen cleared her throat and jumped in before Hugh started in with a rant about hypocrisy. "Sounds like you and Dan The Man have something in common", she said.

"We do, in a way. I mean, both of us lost our dad. But he knew his and I didn't." Jacob said, pointedly.

"That's not what matters honey", Eileen said. "What matters is that you both lost someone you loved, and that loved you. That's a big deal, and now it's something you and Dan share. I hope you guys can talk about that someday "

"Oh we did. Today. I took him to the field to meet dad, and one thing just led to the other, as you say." Satisfied, he started to stuff his mouth again.

Eileen and Old Man smiled at Jacob, and waited for more on the subject. But that was the end of it for the time being.

"I'm going to call his Aunt tonight and make sure she knows that Dan is welcome to come here for Thanksgiving. His mom too", Eileen said then.

"Yeah, I wanna meet her. Did you know she's in prison? And she's an atheist too? I never met an atheist before", Jacob said, matter of factually, downing the last of his milk.

"Okay-Dokey then", was all Eileen could say to that, relieved, but also surprised that he was more interested in someone being an atheist than being in prison. "Anybody want a bowl of ice cream?"

That night, when everyone disappeared into their rooms, Eileen began picking up around the living room, noticing for the second time that day that the doll lay forgotten on the floor beside the large leather chair that was Wife's. Eileen wondered as she picked it up, if Betty's time with her doll, Boy, had come and gone. She placed it in the chair anyway, covering all but its worn cloth head with the afghan.

"Time will tell", she said aloud, turning off the last of the lights, then following the moon's shadow towards the stairway. Climbing-between her cold sheets, Eileen remembered the day her mother brought that very doll home for her and how she'd loved it right off. She chuckled to herself, remembering how she'd named it Lisa, after her best friend who moved away when they were in first grade.

Back then, the painted-on eyes were fresh and blue and the lips were a bright cherry red, the color of ripe fruit right before it falls away from the stem. Her mother bought it from a woman who made and sold craft items to benefit their church. Eileen was glad now that she'd kept it, glad that it still had a purpose and was loved, if even only for a short time.

Then her thoughts drifted to Mary. She'd been so upbeat during their brief phone conversation, given the circumstances facing her. 'Tough lady', she said to herself, then after she turned off the light, she said a little prayer; not to God, but to Aunt Fara.

A MAN CALLED CHOD

The next morning, Old Man got up early and dressed Wife in extra warm clothes, so they could head outside and catch Eliza before she was finished collecting their eggs. He usually avoided this encounter, but now he sought it.

He wanted to secure the things Eileen wanted for the barn, so there would be little left for her to do but enjoy herself. Truth was, he was excited to finally let her see what he'd done to the barn. Soon, he thought.

Eileen was also up by then, groggy and in her pajamas, but up. She didn't question Old Man when they went outside so early. Jacob had another hour before he had to get up and get ready for school, so she drank up the silence of the house.

Pouring a cup of coffee, she sat down to muster up the courage to call Fara. That required a couple of cups of the coal-black liquid. Her curiosity about what was going to happen to Dan The Man was driving her nuts. She cared about what was going to happen to this boy and his poor Aunt, and now with Leila coming home in less than a week, she could only hope Fara would come through. At last, she put down her cup and picked up the phone.

After many rings, a deep voice answered, "Y'ellow?" Surprised that someone other than Fara answered the phone, it took her a few seconds for Eileen to answer. "Morning, this is Eileen Roberts calling. I was wondering if Fara was up and around yet?"

The question brought a deep chuckle from the other end of the line.

"Hello Eileen Roberts, this is Chod. Just happened to hear her phone ringing and ran inside. Didn't mean to throw you off. She's up all right, but long gone, kid."

"Gone already?" Eileen said, surprised. "Would you mind giving me her cell phone number? I need to ask her something."

Another chuckle came through the line. "Cell phone? Fara doesn't have a cell phone." Chod said, clearly amused. "But if you want, I can leave her message and have her call ya back when she gets home. You know, like we used to do in the old days?"

Eileen was amused, but also frustrated. "That'd be fine, thank you. Hey, you don't happen to know where she went do you?" She added quickly.

"Sure do, she went over to Mitchellville to pay a visit to Leila Morgan. Plans on being back here after lunch. Everything okay over there?"

"Yeah everything's fine, Chod, thanks for asking. I just wanted to ask her something, but I guess it'll have to wait. Have a good day and see ya soon."

"Lookin' forward to it, Eileen. Tell Hugh and Betty hello for me", he said as he hung up.

Fara must have something up her sleeve or she wouldn't drive all the way over to Mitchellville, Eileen thought. It's not that she had doubted Fara when she said that something would be done, it's just now she had to wait to find out what that something was, and how she could help.

GRACE COMES IN UNEXPECTED PACKAGES

Already dressed and raring to go, Jacob appeared at her side just as she rang off with Chod. "Morning honey", she said. "Seems everybody's up early today. How about some scrambled eggs and cinnamon toast for breakfast?"

"Sounds good, mom, but give me fifteen minutes, okay? I want to go see dad really quick, and then check in on the girls", he patted his mom on the back as he slipped into his boots and walked out of the house in a hurry.

"Strange", she murmured to herself. "Thing's surely are getting stranger and stranger around here." Then she laughed and made her way into the kitchen to make breakfast.

Jacob passed by the open door to the chicken coop where he saw that three people were crammed inside.

"Morning all", he said, without stopping to ask what they were doing in there. He skipped all the way down the lane, passing the barn, then the stock yard and setting off into the field, following the same tracks he and Dan made the day before.

Arriving at his intended destination, he said to the silent headstone bearing his father's name, "Hey dad, I just wanted to say thanks for yesterday. You being here really helped out my friend." Jacob stood with his hands in his pockets for a couple of minutes before adding, "Well, that's all I wanted to say for now. Got to get ready for school. Love ya." Then he took off, running towards the barn to let his girls out.

On his way back to the house, he noticed the door to the coop was closed and that the three crooked bodies now stood in the driveway talking. He watched his Grandpa, hug Mrs. Reeve, making Jacob wonder if that made his Grandma, the third one of the group, jealous. He let out a puzzled grunt as he slammed into the kitchen.

"What's that noise all about?" His mom asked, as he slipped off his boots.

"Adults are goofy", was all he would say, walking over to the table to dive into his breakfast. "This is really good, thanks mom."

"You're welcome, son, I'm glad you like it. Hey, I'm goin' over to Grandma and Grandpa Erickson's today. Got any messages for them?"

"Yeah, tell them I can't wait to see them on Thanksgiving, okay?"

"You bet", she said, sitting down beside him to finish yet another cup of coffee.

Eliza was gone by the time Eileen and Jacob left the house. Old Man stood at the back of his truck, assessing the contents in its bed, when the two walked up.

He leaned against the open tailgate where Wife sat, dangling her legs. He was no doubt protecting her from falling off. She wore his coat on top of hers, a hat and the familiar blank stare.

It didn't matter to Eileen or Jacob that she didn't look their way, or acknowledge their approach. All that mattered, to people who loved her was that she was safe and content, and she was clearly both. The skinny legs that rocked back from the tailgate with ease confirmed it.

"What's up, you two?" Eileen asked, walking towards her car.

"Talked to Eliza this morning, and she said we could go over anytime to pick up the things you asked for." Old Man answered.

Patting Wife on the leg, and looking up at the sky, he added, "I thought today would be a good day for a drive, but first I have to clean out some of this junk", he said, pointing to the back of his truck. "Sure would like to get it all in one load."

"That's awesome Hugh, thanks a ton. Breakfast is on the table and I'll be home around noon. I'm goin' over to mom and dads for a while. You two be careful", she said, feeling some concern. She knew they hadn't been away from the farm in quite a while, but she also knew her place, and it wasn't to give this man advice or lecture him about being careful. The pecking order hadn't changed just because she was living there. Old Man was her elder and the man of the house. She would always be respectful of that.

"Bye, Grandpa, bye Grandma", Jacob said, closing the car door behind him, and off they went.

Fara had been at Mitchellville for less than an hour, before she and Leila came up with a plan for Dan the Man's immediate future. With her job there finished, they hugged, and then Leila was led away from the visitor's room by a friendly female guard. Fara noticed how easily the guard and Leila talked as they disappeared through a large steel doorway. They seemed more like friends than prisoner and guard.

Fara turned towards the exit door meant for visitors, but as she made her way towards it, a tough looking inmate in a white t-shirt and prison issued orange pants leaned against the wall, giving Fara the once over.

"I need a cigarette", the woman barked at Fara.

"Yeah, and people in hell need ice water too", Fara said, never missing a step as she passed the inmate and the guard, the latter of whose face broke into a large smile. "Amen, sister", the guard said to Fara's back as she locked the door behind her.

Back in Ottumwa, Eileen's dad, Bob, was busy playing bridge in the Silver Woods great room when she arrived.

"Hey sugar", he said, looking up when she took a place at his side. After her dad proudly introduced his daughter to the other 'guys' at the table, she kissed his head and said, "Good luck", then made her way down the pastel-colored hallway to her parents' unit.

Inside her parent's new digs, Eileen, sat admiring the way her mother had made the small space, they now called home cozy, while her mother busied herself making coffee. Not that Eileen needed any more coffee, but she wasn't going to be a party pooper and spoil her mom's good intentions.

Eileen was so glad that her parents seemed settled and content in their new surroundings. It was a load off her shoulders, which she knew had been part of their plan, even if they wouldn't admit to it. She loved them for that, and for so many thousands of other reasons.

"What are your plans for tomorrow, mom?" She asked.

"Why, what's up hon?" Her mother asked.

"I just thought you might want to come out and help me decorate the barn. It'll be fun, just you and me. Dad can come too if he wants, but there isn't going to be any job for him to do."

"That's perfect, because he doesn't want a job", Katherine said, chuckling "He can visit with Hugh, though, How's Betty doing?"

"That's a hard one to answer", Eileen sighed. "She's doing all right, considering. However, I think she's moved into another stage of her dementia."

"What does that mean, a 'stage'?" Katherine asked.

Eileen explained. "Like with Alzheimer's, in the beginning a person begins to lose details, dates, names, appointments, and so on. Then, as the disease progresses and consumes more of their short-term memory, what's left are mostly memories of long ago, like childhood, and only fragments at that. The medical world calls the progression 'stages,' which gives us some idea of what's next, and what to expect. It's never good. It takes years sometimes, for those around them to notice what's happening, because we assume 'forgetting' is a normal thing for someone getting older. Imagine all the people living alone that have no family at all, or no family active, day to day in their lives. Think how long they suffer before any intervention takes place."

"Try to imagine, mom", Eileen said, now with tears in her eyes, "walking outside of your house and becoming lost in your own front yard. Some people wander off and are never found because no one knows they are missing. And they can't call anyone because they don't remember anyone to call."

Katherine shuddered.

"Betty's been lost many times, but so far, Hugh's always found her. He dresses her, takes her to the bathroom, wipes her butt, feeds her and so on, and has been doing all of this for a very long time, all by himself. He is familiar to her, only because he's been the constant presence in her life, not because she knows who he is. Having someone familiar is no small thing in that strange world."

"She doesn't know me or Jacob, and we don't care. Jacob's so smart, mom. He treats her no differently than he always has. I think it's safe to say, that Betty's in the late stages of dementia, which means soon she won't be able to function at all. We just started pureeing her food, so she doesn't choke. You see, she doesn't remember how to swallow.... I think we moved out there at just the right time. Hugh needs my help."

"You're' awfully sweet, ya know that?" Her mom said, smiling at her daughter.

"It's all sweet", Eileen said, "but also sad at the same time. I wish

I could tell you some of the things that happen around there, but I wouldn't do them justice if I tried. Just believe me when I say that, every now and then, a small miracle takes place. Betty goes from saying nothing for days, then all of a sudden, she'll say one word or do one thing and we all understand its meaning. That little bit of something tickles us, and makes Hugh so happy. He has changed a great deal in the past few weeks. It's amazing to watch."

"What's amazing honey, is how powerful and important love is." Katherine said. "I think that's why some of us old people get older faster and fade away quicker. I've seen it happen to people I've known my whole life. There's nothing to keep 'em going. That's why they say animals make such a difference in older people's lives. They're something to love and be loved. It's a proven fact! I'm so darn proud of you, Eileen. Charly would be too."

"Thanks mom, I think he would", she said, taking one last sip of coffee. But mid-sip, Eileen's phone rang, interrupting their conversation. She looked at the caller ID. "Excuse me mom, I'm expecting this call", she said as she got up from the table and went into the living room area to the couch.

The caller ID said, 'Kremer.' "Hello?" Eileen answered.

"Y'ellow", came back. It was the same deep voice as before. "Eileen?"

"Yes, this is Eileen. Is this Chod?"

"How'd ya know it was me?" He asked, surprised.

"I'm psychic", Eileen declared, not feeling the need to explain caller ID or that his way of saying, 'Y'ello,' tipped her off. "What's up Chod, Fara back yet?" She asked.

"She is, and she asked me to call you so you don't fret. Those were her exact words. 'Don't fret.' Said you'd know what she was gettin' at. Anyway, I was calling to ask you if your boy could come to the ranch after school to help me and Dude out with some new calves? Already asked Mary if her nephew could come out too. I'd be happy to pick him up at school if it's okay. We'll feed him when we're done, and bring him home before it's too late. Whatta'ya think?"

"Well, it's kind of short notice, but I guess it's okay. I'll call the school and let them know that you'll be picking him up. Don't have him out too late, 'ya hear?" She added.

"Got it, and thanks, kid", he said. Then he hung up, again without saying goodbye.

During the call, Katherine motioned to Eileen that she would be right back and left the unit to check on 'the guys'. Eileen stayed seated on the couch with its noisy plastic covered cushions and waited for her mother to return, all the while wondering what was up with the Kremers. They had never asked Jacob to their ranch before. Something was up all right, she was sure of it. She was also pretty darn sure that Aunt Fara was behind whatever it was.

With Jacob working after school, she figured she might as well take advantage of the free time that afforded. So, she decided that after visiting her mother, she'd stop by Sarah's place. There was something she wanted to find out from her too.

As Eileen turned into Sarah's long driveway, she noticed how the morning's blue sky was quickly clouding over, disguising the time of day. Snow threatened, and she kicked herself for not bringing a jacket along. She was just about to get out of her car when she caught movement out of the corner of her eye.

She saw two riders on horses way across the pasture, both with long flowing hair that danced up and down as they rode. At first it looked like two women, but after a few minutes she recognized Austen and Sarah.

She'd never seen Austen without a hat on, except for when he was a little kid. Back then, everything about him was short, hair included.

She laughed out loud, remembering what a funny kid he'd been, always pulling pranks of one kind or another on her when she babysat. He was gifted with a sense of humor, something Eileen didn't believe could be taught or bought, like common sense. It was something a person was either born with or without, and Austen had both. As far as she was concerned, he was perfect for Sarah.

She watched as the two rode fast and hard, maneuvering around and around each other, as only experienced riders could. They reminded her of skilled barrel racing events at the rodeos. She sat in her car, enjoying the show without their knowledge, for about ten minutes before it hit her.

"Riding lessons, my ass. You sly dog, Austen", she mumbled out loud.

She had come out there clearly to snoop, with the main goal of setting them up if possible. But they'd beaten her to the punch. It was obvious they had a thing for each other, something she could plainly see from her car.

She felt like a window peeper, but she couldn't have been happier and wondered as she headed home whether old Eliza wasn't the only one deserving of the name 'snoopy pants'.

Feeling awkward and nervous, Chod and Dude walked into Hoak Elementary school together to retrieve the boys they'd been sent to pick up. They stood outside the office doors, having left their names with the school secretary. She looked them up and down suspiciously when they told her who they were there to pick up, even making them show their
104

driver's license to prove who they were.

When the bell rang, what looked like a swarm of midgets came running from all directions, some heading for the same door where the big men waited patiently.

Dude said to Chod, "I feel like a giant in here."

"In that green coverall you're wearin' I'd say you look like the Jolly Green Giant", Chod shot back.

They chuckled, but their eyes never left the hordes of little people running by them.

Then, out of nowhere, two young boys wearing grins as wide as the Raccoon River appeared in front of them.

"Ready to roll?" Chod asked the boys.

"You bet we are, sir", Dan The Man answered.

"Let's hit it!" Jacob added, without hesitation.

The secretary watched through the window as the four climbed into the large blue diesel truck, and wrote the license plate numbers down before it pulled away, just in case.

Ten minutes later, Mary walked into the office and checked the sign out sheet. She smiled to herself as she read the names. She stayed away from their rendezvous spot on purpose, even though it was hard thing for her to do. She was controlling and she knew it. And, she'd admit that maybe she was even a little too strict with her nephew. But she loved him so. All she'd ever meant to do was protect him.

Now, she was losing control. Their lives were taking a turn not of her choosing, and she knew that she had to have faith and trust in those around her.

When Fara called that morning, to ask her if it was okay if Dan came out to the ranch after school, she'd also kindly reminded her that not everything was hers to decide. She suggested holding off telling Dan about his mother having to leave again, and to wait for Leila to come home so that she could talk to her son first.

Before Fara said goodbye, she assured Mary that things would work out. Fara had a way of convincing a person of that, for which Mary was more than grateful. As hard as it was for her to not control everything, she was taking Fara's advice, even admitting to herself that not being in control was a welcomed relief.

Dan had been so excited when she told him the Kremers needed a ranch hand, and that they wanted to give him a shot at it. He needed men in his life, good men, and if he happened to learn how to work hard in the process, that would be icing on the cake.

It was time for Mary to go home, and with Dan away for dinner, maybe even run a hot bath and drink a glass of wine. It was time for her to let go and worry about herself for a change.

Snow had begun to fall, by the time Eileen arrived back at the farm. The rooftops were covered in white, as were the vast open fields. The heavy wet snow clung to random boards on the buildings and gray smoke billowed and curled its way out of the barn's chimney, reminding her of a Christmas card.

Eileen smiled, thinking how Old Man was always one step ahead of her. The smoke and the four-wheeler tracks, even though they were being erased by the snow, now, gave him away.

She followed the tracks to the barn and entered slowly and quietly through the large doors. It was warm and toasty inside, just like Old Man had said it would be. He was on the opposite end of the barn near the stove, stacking firewood into a neat pile, Wife sat close by on a bale of hay, watching him. They hadn't noticed her yet, so she hung a left to say hello to the bedded calves. When she turned back around, she almost tripped over the pumpkins piled into one of the vacant stalls, and next to that pile was another one of corn stalks and random varieties of squash in all of the colors of autumn.

At that moment, Eileen didn't think life could get any better than it was, that is, until she rounded the posts by the stalls and faced the center of the barn. There, four beautiful pine tables stood, with matching benches tucked up underneath them. The tables were long and narrow, designed to seat many. They reminded her of the family tables she'd seen in a few Amish homes.

There would be no wobbly pop up tables, and no folding chairs to separate guests from one another during their Thanksgiving feast. Her guests would sit shoulder to shoulder as they talked, and ate and drank, until the only thing left for them to do was dance.

A squeal of delight came from deep within her, making Old Man jump and turn away from the woodpile. Wife never flinched.

With open arms, he yelled out to Eileen, "Surprise!" Sending echoes through the large space, like a stone being skipped across water.

Eileen came running to him like a child, landing right into his arms. "I love it! I love it! I love it!" She cried.

Only then did Betty look away from the pile of firewood and, with no one watching, stood up and shuffled through the tangled straw and dirt to where the two stood and joined them in a group hug.

"Yep, it doesn't get any better than this", Eileen said, hugging the two.

BOY

When the weather turned nasty, I decided to head inside. My buddies were already inside, taking up all of the available nests, which means I won't be sleeping alone tonight. Again.

I'm not complaining, it's just that sleeping light to avoid being smooshed gets old.

Anyway, so there I was, perched up high and minding my own business, while I dried off my feathers. The only noise other than a coo or two was The Furry One, crawling around under our house, hunting I assumed, when all of a sudden out of the corner of my eye I see something come in through MY hole in the wall!

I teetered, almost falling off my perch. For a moment I thought I'd been wrong and maybe it wasn't The Furry One I heard under the house, but the bogey man.

I've heard stories about the ruthless weasel that kills whatever it can, but so far, I've been lucky. I haven't seen him around. The others tell me how he steals their eggs when they're not looking.

Rotten, rotten bogey man!

And then I saw her. It wasn't the bogey man making noise. Not at all, but someone that looked a lot like me, but prettier.

She came in through my hole and landed on the window sill next to my stash of seed, shaking the wet snow from her body all over it.

Trust me, I didn't mind. And if you could've seen her, you wouldn't have minded either.

FARM HAND

Chod stood in the middle of one of the many rutted roads on the ranch facing in the direction of his new employees headed towards him. He waved both arms to get their attention. "Time to go, you can stop now", he yelled at them, with no visible effect on either of the boys.

Once they'd finished shoveling manure out of one of the barns, Dude promoted them to dumping feed in the troughs along the fence line. It was slow work, but had the allure of driving a small tractor around. The boys were oblivious to anything other than whose turn it was to drive, so the cattle were lining up faster than they could drop the feed.

Dude had expected as much. He knew he'd be the one to finish up after they'd left, which was fine by him.

Both men were surprised at how much they enjoyed the boys' company; they had no expectations when they picked them up from school a few hours before. The mission for the day, which they would soon be sharing with Fara, was accomplished.

Chod jumped in his Ranger and headed down to where the tractor crept along the side of the road. The two boys didn't even look over when he pulled up beside them.

"Hey!" Chod called out, startling them, but definitely getting their attention. "Time to go boys. I promised everyone we'd have you home early, and I intend to keep that promise. I don't wanna' make anyone mad on your first day of work, now turn the tractor around and park it alongside the pole barn where you got it, ya' hear?"

"Yes, sir", they answered in unison.

Chod pulled away, watching them from the rear-view mirror. He chuckled when he saw them instantly begin the Rock-Paper-Scissor thing to determine who got to drive the tractor back to the barn. It was a game he remembered from his own childhood, and it tickled him to know that it wasn't obsolete, like so many other things.

Jacob must have won, because Chod saw him grab hold of the steering wheel before Dan's butt even cleared the seat.

When Dan and Jacob got home from work that night, they smelled like shit. Literally. But each wore a smile that no one could've stole away from either of them.

Independently, and at their own homes, the first question out of their mouths was, "When can I work again?"

Eileen was thrilled that her son was so excited, because it meant that the boys were getting along. She was certain that Mary felt the same way, but with Thanksgiving now only three days away, Eileen decided 'work' was going to have to wait until the long holiday weekend. That didn't please Jacob, nor did it shut him up. She listened from the kitchen as Jacob told his Grandpa about how he got to drive a tractor, and when she butted in to object to someone his age driving anything with a motor in it, Old Man held up his hand to quiet her. Frustrated, but noticing the serious look on his face, she heard him out.

"I was driving a truck 'round this farm when I was his age. Course I couldn't drive it on the road, but around the farm was okay. That's how I learned to drive. I think I was seven or eight, even younger than Jacob. This boy has to learn sometime, honey, because I'm counting on him to help me out in the fields this spring."

Jacob sat next to his Grandpa, nodding his head up and down in agreement. There was no arguing with them, not now anyway, so Eileen shut right up, making the motion of buttoning up her lips, which made them smile. She would take the subject up with Dude and Chod later, before Jacob's next 'job'.

At the Ashley home, things were very much the same, except that when Dan asked when he could work again, his Aunt said, "Tomorrow's fine. The guys will pick you up from school, just like they did today. Now go git in the shower and wash that crap off of you!"

Dan walked over to Mary and looked up at her. "Thanks, Aunt Mary, for everything you do for me." Then he was gone.

She had waited a long time to hear those words, but hadn't figured she'd hear them until he grew into a man and reflected on the time they'd spent together. Now, she only hoped she would live long enough to see him become a man.

Mary knew the plan. Fara told her what she had in store for Dan, and

it was better than the plan she had, which was no plan at all. He would go out to the Kremer ranch every day but Thanksgiving. His mom would be home soon, and she could talk to him about the next eight months. Hopefully, by then he would be open to moving to the ranch to live with Chod and Dude, at least until his mom came home for good, or until she came home from Des Moines. She crossed her fingers, and even looked down at them for extra luck before she warmed Dan's supper.

Old Man fed the calves for Jacob, and reminded him during supper that his new job couldn't get in the way of his chores. Jacob said he understood, and thanked his Grandpa for feeding them just this once.

After he was done eating, he wanted to say hello and goodnight to his critters. "I'll be right back, mom", he said, heading outside with a flashlight.

"I guess it's time for bed", Old Man said to Wife, who was already fast asleep in her chair. Before he got up from the table, Eileen remembered to tell him that her parents would be coming over in the morning.

She was excited to begin the decorating. So much so, that she really didn't care at this point who helped her. The barn was going to be perfect, no matter what, thanks to Hugh.

"That'll be just fine honey. Haven't seen them in a while. Your dad has always got a few good stories to tell, and I've been saving up my BS for months." With a chuckle, he turned to his wife. "Okay then, woman, let's go on to bed. You got a big day tomorrow."

Wife woke up as he lifted her from the chair, and as he did, he looked around for her baby, but it was nowhere to be found. So be it, as long as she wasn't missing him, he decided to let it go.

Eileen watched them enter the bathroom and heard the facet squeak.

Over the sound of water, she swore she heard laughter, but then Jacob came running in, pulling her attention away from the bathroom and whatever private joke that was going on inside of it.

"I see you've found your surprise, mom", Jacob said, pulling off his dirty clothes at the door, until he had nothing left on, but his Incredible Hulk underwear.

"I sure did, and I hear you had something to do with it", she smiled.

Jacob walked over to his mom at the table and put his arms around her neck.

"We wanted to make you happy, mom, and I'm sooooo glad it worked!" He said.

When he released his grip on her, she kissed his cheek. "It worked all right. Now, as soon as the bathroom's free, I want you to wash that crap off of you. You stink!" She scolded with a grin.

"Dang", he said, as he walked into his bedroom.

The next day, the boys bragged to their classmates, and anyone else that would listen, about having driven a tractor at their 'job.' Some of the kids didn't believe them, which made the story grow and morph into more than it had been, and though they shared in the notoriety they were creating, Jacob couldn't help but be jealous that Dan was getting to go to work that day without him.

He envisioned Dan driving the tractor around all by himself, but tried not to show his annoyance. To deal with it, he flirted with Kary Lynn, a classmate that Dan just happened to have a crush on.

Flirting at this age meant he teased her, about whatever a guy could think of ,which wasn't much, but in this case, Dan took notice.

Lucky for the kids, a substitute teacher happened to be in the class-room that day, and as everyone knows, no matter the era, the unspoken rule is that you can take advantage of subs. And they did. Some kids talked back and forth from desk to desk, while others milled around the room, as if the teacher was invisible.

Dan interrupted Jacob's conversation with Kary Lynn, shouting from across the room, and trying with what little he had to steal her attention away from his new friend.

"Hey Kary Lynn, what are you doin' for Thanksgiving?" He called out.

Kary Lynn flipped her hair from side to side, loving the double attention

"I'm going to the Roberts' farm with my family", she answered.

Both boys looked at each other in surprise, and before either of them could say anything, Beth, who was on the other side of the room, piped in, "I'll be there too!"

Beth was a little girl with long brown hair and big brown eyes to match. She had shown interest in Jacob before, which until that moment he could have cared less about. Girls were still 'gross' in his opinion, but for some reason the look she now gave him made him warm all over. He wondered what the heck was happening to him as he moved away from Kary Lynn and walked across the room to 'brown eyes'.

In no time, Kary Lynn and Dan followed him over. The four kids huddled together like they were members of a prestigious club, "The Thanksgiving Club." Kary Lynn attempted to 'one up' the rest of them by talking about how her parent's band was going to be the entertainment for the festivities. But then Peter, or Booger Eater as he was known since kindergarten, interrupted.

Smugly scooting his chair over to the group, he said, "Hey, my family's coming too! My mom's the fiddle player and everyone knows you can't have a Bluegrass band without a fiddle player."

Kary Lynn had been trumped. She rolled her eyes at Booger Eater, but left the subject of who was the most valued band member alone. She didn't want to argue, only brag.

Jacob thought about adding his two cents, but decided against it, noticing how Beth seemed disinterested in a pissing contest. He liked her more because she didn't want to participate.

But Dan did want to jump in, wanting to tell everyone about his mother coming home, and how she would be at the Roberts' farm for Thanksgiving, just like everyone else. But an unfamiliar apprehension stopped him. For the first time, it crossed Dan's mind that others might have questions or opinions about his mother, and he was in no mood to hear them. He would, however, defend her tooth and nail, if and when the time came.

The kids talked on about music and dancing, and how they planned to eat until they were sick. Then the bell rang, emptying the room out like magic.

Dan was eager to see Chod and Dude again, but he also knew that it bothered Jacob that he got to go to work without him. For the first time in his life he had a true friend, and he didn't want a dumb tractor to come between them. So, he jogged down the hallway and caught Jacob at his locker.

"Hey dude, don't worry. Friday, you can drive the tractor all day if you want. And just for you, I'll shovel the shit."

Jacob's face lit up. 'Girls smirls', he thought, as he hand bumped Dan's fist. Friends were way better. "Thanks", he said. And he meant it.

When Dan arrived with Chod and Dud that day, they passed a young boy on a tractor, the same tractor Dan and Jacob drove the day before. Dan jerked his head towards the back window and asked, "Who's that?"

"That's John Ray, he works out here sometimes." Dude said as he drove the big truck up the dirt road.

"He looks like a Mexican", Dan said, watching the kid dump feed along the fence line like a pro.

Dude didn't respond to Dan's comment, but Chod, sitting in the passenger seat, did.

"We have a few Mexicans working here, and I got to tell ya' son, they're some of the hardest workers we have. Whad'ya think of that?"

"I'm not sure what to think about that", he answered, as honestly as a ten-year-old could.

"Many of the Mexicans round here are migrant workers", Chod went on. "Know what a migrant worker is, Dan?"

"No", the boy answered, turning his face away from the window to face the back of the talking heads in the front seat.

"A migrant worker is someone who follows the seasons of crops, picking fruit and vegetables mainly. They hand pick the crops, which is grueling work. Sometimes entire families work in the fields together, harvesting a crop of one kind or another, and the majority of them just happen to be Mexican", Chod said.

Dude added, "There's a town few hundred miles from here called Muscatine, known for its musk melons. Know who the majority are that live in that town, boy? Mexicans, that's who. And why is that? Because a long time ago, they migrated there to pick melons and other things. Many of them stayed and made it their home."

Dude went on to explain that migrant workers travel from state to state, crop to crop working long hours in the hot sun for wages most other people are "too good" to work for.

"Hell, do you know if it wasn't for Mexicans we wouldn't have fruit or vegetables in our markets?"

"What are you saying, that white people are lazy?" Dan asked, in all sincerity.

Deep laughter came from the front seat, from both men.

"No, that's not at all what I'm saying", Dude said. "Lazy comes in all colors. What I am saying is that most people - okay, a lot of people - are too proud to work for low wages. It just turns out that a lot of those folks are white."

"Pride can be a funny thing, boy. And I don't mean ha-ha funny. Some folks' pride comes from being able to support their families, even if it means they have to work more than one job to do it. While others think

112

they're too good to work those same jobs. Instead, they sit on their butts and collect welfare. Tell me, where's the pride in that, boy?"

Feeling like the conversation might be getting too deep for a ten year-old, Chod butted in. "Okay, okay, the bottom line is this. If you are a hard worker, you will never go hungry, nor will your children. You might not have the newest cars or the latest fashion in clothes, but you'll never go hungry, and in our opinion, that's something to be proud of. Now on that note, let's get to work!"

The three of them climbed out of the truck as soon as it came a stop, and headed to the main barn so Dan could change into his work clothes. On their way in, Dude asked Dan, "I hear your mama's coming home soon?"

Dan's face brightened. "Yep, she'll be home tonight! I can hardly wait."

Dan immediately smelled smoking meat when he walked into the barn, making his stomach grumble in hunger. It was the sausage hanging in the smoke house, getting smoked to perfection for the Thanksgiving feast. It sure smelled better than the manure he would soon be shoveling.

The men walked over to the work bench and appeared to start fiddling with a small motor, but they were watching the boy and giving each other conspiratorial winks.

Dan leaned against a wall to take off his tennis shoes, then he pulled up the coveralls his Aunt Mary bought him from the thrift store. Once that was on and zipped up, he put on his work boots and waited for instruction.

On cue, Aunt Fara came walking out of the small room off the barn, known as "the office. "Her pipe dangled from her lips. "Hey you", she said, walking casually over, and giving Dan's shoulder a squeeze. "How's work treatin' ya' so far?"

Her jacket smelled of tobacco, adding to the other wonderful aromas in the barn.

"So far so good, Aunt Fara", he said, as they stood eye to eye. She wasn't much taller than he was, so it was easy to do that. "I can't wait to start making real money. Allowances don't count ya' know, as 'real' money. Hey, when do I get paid anyway?" He asked, boldly.

Chod and Dude turned around when the subject of payday came up, and Dan instantly regretted his question. They saw their recent lesson in pride flash across his little pea brain, and his face turned red as a beet, making both men smile with satisfaction.

Suddenly, Dan realized that what those men thought of him mattered, and right before he could back-pedal, Fara jumped in and saved him.

"You'll get paid once a week, like everyone else round here, but you won't get paid unless you earn it, get it?" Fara said looking back into the big eyes that stared back at her.

"Got it" Dan said, meaning it.

"What're you going to do with all that money anyway?" Fara asked, humoring the kid.

The boy jumped on that so fast, one would've thought he'd been making a list. "First I'm going to buy my mom some new clothes. She can't go around town in those orange things she's been wearing. Then I'm going to take my mom and Aunt Mary to Big D's Steak house. Then I'm going to save up for a dirt bike. Then I might put some in the bank. Then I'm…"

Fara could tell that his list of wants was long, and could possibly go on forever, but daylight was a-burning, so she interrupted him "Well, you're in luck, son, 'cause we're going to be short a hand here real soon and we'll be needing another good one. That means you'll have plenty of money to buy what you want. But right now, you're going to be cleaning out the office", Fara said, pointing to it.

"It's one hell of a mess. When you're done in there you can go home, take a few days off for the holiday. But, after Thanksgiving, it's back to work. That sound okay to you?"

"Sounds good to me, Aunt Fara", he said, thinking about how he couldn't wait for the day to be over so he could get home and see his mom.

Fara and the men watched Dan walk across the room to the office door, wearing a pair of coveralls that bore someone else's name across the back, maneuvering around farm equipment and miscellaneous parts along the way. They knew he was anticipating seeing a terrible mess inside the empty room, but they also knew something else.

Fara unconsciously grabbed hold of her two brothers' hands as Dan went for the doorknob, and when the squeal of surprise and delight came pouring out of that room they knew it was time for them to go.

Before they'd made it to the exit door they heard, "Mom you're here! You're really here! Then, "Hey, where'd ya' get those new clothes?"

ALMOST THANKSGIVING

Back at the Roberts' farm, Eileen and Katherine had just finished decorating the center of the tables with Eliza's donated harvest. Pumpkins,

Indian corn, and an occasional gourd highlighted the beautiful wooden tables that stretched the length of the barn.

The posts were dressed in cornstalk bundles, and the simple bandstand was now encircled and defined by hay bales. The only thing left to do was disguise the raft of card tables in white sheets where the food and drink would be placed.

For most of the morning, Betty sat next to the wood stove with her eyes glued to the stack of wood piled up in front of her. Only once did she leave her warm, safe spot, shuffling over to the dwindling pile of corn near the calves' pen.

Eileen didn't intervene, but she did stop what she was doing, just in case. The barn floor was uneven, and a shuffler ran the risk of falling.

Eileen watched Betty bend down on one knee and feed Bob, and then Daisy, each an ear of corn, one at a time, through the slats in their pens. She was a natural.

It was no secret that feeding and caring for the animals was once her favorite part of rural life, a passion she shared and passed on to her son, Charly.

Eileen briefly entertained the idea of getting more animals for Betty, as a type of medicine, but as soon as that thought entered her head, she saw that bewildered look return to Betty's face. Her eyes began to search the very same barn she'd spent most of her life in for something familiar. Seeing her bewilderment was ugly and sad, all at the same time.

Dementia was not going to let her stay in this world or the old one. Like a hungry monster, it would not be satisfied until it gobbled her all up.

In the short time it took Eileen to walk over and lead Betty back to the warm seat by the stove, she was a once again a shell of a woman, willing to be led anywhere by anyone.

Katherine had called it quits for the day, and watched her daughter from one of the benches. She was proud of the woman her little girl had become, but also terrified to witness the decline of the once sharp and vibrant Betty Lou.

After Betty was seated and safe, Eileen climbed a ladder near the stove and hung orange crepe paper along the rafters above, not taking notice of the two birds that hopped along the old timbers in front of her hands.

When she finished, she folded the ladder and set it up against a wall, then sat down next to her mother to admire the colors surrounding them.

The barn and the tables looked incredible, better than you'd find in the Thanksgiving addition of Country Living. It was totally ready for guests.

After a few minutes, Hugh and Bob walked into the barn, each carrying a bottle of Pabst Blue Ribbon in their hand. Katherine's eyes instantly zeroed in on the beers, and she 'mean mugged' her husband on his way to the table.

Once upon a time, Bob drank too much, and for thirty-some odd years his wife threatened to leave him because of it. Then one day, out of the blue, he just quit drinking, never admitting to anyone including himself that it had been a problem.

In truth, it was his age that motivated him, not consequences or his wife's repeated threats. Like many who crest that hill, he simply woke up one day and acknowledged that his life was almost over, and with deep clarity, decided to be a sober part of it.

Of course, Katherine was happy when he quit; actually, more relieved than happy. Sadly, though, by this point in their lives she had a whole lot of anger and resentment stored up, and it didn't just disappear with the drinking. It was something she consciously worked on because she loved the man.

Seeing her face, Bob instantly felt the need to defend himself. "Somethin' about a holiday makes a man feel like he's not on any schedule, and can do whatever he wants to do. Isn't that right, Hugh?"

"That's right, buddy", Hugh said, stopping to take a drink from his bottle.

"Like you are ever on any schedule?" Katherine said, forcing a chuckle. "Just so you don't get tuned up, dear. I have lots of cooking to do tonight, and I need you to be sober enough to drive us home!"

"Not to worry, this isn't my first rodeo, nor is it my last", he added with sheepish smile, proud that he'd held his ground, even though it wasn't necessary.

"So, what do you think, guys?" Eileen asked, motioning around the room.

"It's beautiful" Hugh said, searching the room for Wife and finding her near the wood stove, eyes fixed on the firewood stacked the day before.

He thought she looked pale, but the lighting was spotty. It wasn't until he walked up right alongside of her that he knew there was no question about her color, there was none.

The others sat talking while Old Man sat his half empty bottle of beer down between a couple of pieces of split wood. When he turned back around, he saw Boy standing on Wife's left shoulder.

Wife didn't look at Old Man. Nor did she acknowledge the bird that had not long ago had been her Boy, their savior.

He gently scooted the bird off her shoulder, realizing how he hadn't thought about it for a while, not since Wife's attention switched over to the doll, the doll that she no longer searched for either.

He watched the bird fly above them and land on the rafter next to another bird that looked just like him. Hugh was glad the little guy had found a friend, and glad that his wife, despite all her misery, had insisted on saving him. In turn, the bird had given them gifts that, in his mind, were nothing short of miracles.

Before tending to Wife, he gave thanks to the bird called 'Boy.'

"I think it's time for a nap", he said, lifting her up from her seat, and guiding her through the straw and dirt towards the door. Just then, Jacob walked in.

"Hi Grandpa, hi Grandma", he said. Then, "Bye Grandpa, bye Grandma."

"Hi son", Old Man said. "We'll be in the house if ya' need us."

At long last, it was finally the day before Thanksgiving and almost everyone who'd been invited to the Roberts' for Thanksgiving was either on their way to work or on their way to school, all hoping for a short day.

The guests who were retired from jobs were more than likely home, getting a jump on their contributions to the feast. But, regardless of age or occupation, all were anticipating a great day ahead.

THE AHSLEY/MORGAN HOME

Dan asked his mother to pick him up after school and drive him to Comanche for, "Just a minute."

When she asked him why he wanted to go there, he said, very matter of factly, "There's something I want to talk to dad about."

Leila was caught off guard, so she looked to her sister for a hint, anything that could assist with an answer.

Mary was busy gathering the papers she'd graded the night before and was cramming them into her pack. She looked up and met her sister's eyes, but didn't offer any clues or assistance in the matter.

She just shrugged her shoulders and smiled. She'd decided to take a backseat for the next few days and intervene only if it was really needed.

Mary knew that Leila still had the burden of telling her son that she would be leaving after Thanksgiving. Time was short between mother and son, so she was staying out of their business, as hard as it was for her to do.

For once, she was relieved to be going to school.

It was as if Leila read her mind.

She turned back to her son, who waited for an answer. How about this, honey. How about you don't go to school today, and we go wherever you want to go. That is, unless you want to go to school?"

Dan automatically looked over to his Aunt for permission. She was the rule-maker, the enforcer of everything in his life. She winked to let him know it was okay, feeling a little guilty that he looked to her for permission. She felt a tug on her heart. She loved him like he was her own. She couldn't help it. It's just what happens when you take care of a child and make them the priority of your life.

And like everything that involves love, heartache is part of what you sign up for, whether or not you know it at the time.

Mary had known the day that she'd have to let go of Dan would come. But though her head told her she was prepared for it, her heart was calling her head a liar.

"You think I am crazy? 'Course I don't want to go to school. I want to spend the day with you, mom!"

Dan looked over to his Aunt again, "Thanks, Aunt Mary", he said.

"You're welcome", Mary chuckled. "I'll see you two this evening." Then she quickly disappeared through the doorway.

"If we leave right now we can eat at that pancake house in Comanche-remember, the place with the huge pancakes and all the sausage gravy a person could ever want?" Dan asked excitedly.

"Of course I remember it. 'Annie's' was our favorite spot. Sure baby, that sounds good. And after you've talked to your dad maybe you and I can talk for a while."

"I'm so glad you're home, mom", Dan said, hugging his mother. "I'm so glad you're home!"

Trying to clear the lump in her throat, she whispered, "Me too, now let's go see if that car of ours will start."

SARAH'S STABLES

Meanwhile, over at Sarah's, the pecan pies were all baked and cooling on the porch, set high enough up that her two dogs, or any other critters, couldn't help themselves to a treat. At least she hoped they couldn't.

She'd already shot two squirrels that had looked at the porch suspiciously, and though she really didn't want to shoot any more of them, she would to protect the pies she'd spent all morning making.

She leaned her 22 rifle against the house and stepped down from the porch. She needed to get Johnny, one of her favorite horses, saddled and ready to ride. She didn't have any lessons today, but she did have a guest coming out to ride.

Austen would soon be arriving with his own horse and trailer. The day before they had decided to take a long ride down gravel roads, just to see how their horses would do together. If everything went as planned, they'd ride the back roads to the Roberts' farm the following day for Thanksgiving.

On her way to the stable, she stuck out her tongue, licking random snowflakes from the air and thinking as she did how the new falling snow made everything more romantic. Her anticipation over her handsome guest's arrival made her feel more alive than she'd ever felt before.

If their test ride was a success, which Sarah was certain it would be, they would take her pies, along with whatever wild rice concoction Austen made, to the Roberts' in his truck later that evening. That way, they wouldn't have to worry about the impossible task of packing their food by horseback the next day.

She was excited for many reasons, but most of all she was excited to be the 'pilgrim' that this particular Indian chose to go with for a Thanksgiving dinner.

HEINS' HOG FARM

Mike and Evert Heins' smoke house had been filled to capacity for the past two days, overflowing with young turkeys and hams, raised and butchered by the Heins themselves.

The smoke that filled the air was blinding, like a fog that wouldn't lift. As the dead fields wept, those lucky enough to be outside could catch a whiff of Thanksgiving on the breeze.

The inside of the house held wonderful smells of its own, thanks to Mike's wife, Debra. Her oyster stuffing was 'to-die-for,' But, because she'd once owned her own restaurant and was licensed in food safety. Her instincts told her to call Eileen and let her know that the stuffing she was bringing was full of fresh oysters. In the event that someone at the feast had a shellfish allergy, she didn't want anyone to actually die from eating her stuffing.

Food allergies were something you never thought about in the old days. You just ate what was served and found out later if it made you sick. But times change.

Evert's wife, Barbara, had been gone five years now, and if it hadn't been for his son and daughter-in-law, he would've given up on holidays all together.

Pastor Dale told him a few years back, while trying to talk him into spending Thanksgiving with him and his wife, Linda Rae, that family are those you surround yourself with, "whether or not they're blood."

But it wasn't until this moment, as he removed the meat from the smoker and transferred it into the large cooler in his barn, that he understood what his pastor meant.

In his heart, he'd always known that people he called friends were a part of him, close enough to consider family. He was excited for the next day, excited to be able to share his bounty with the people he cared for and loved.

THE GRAHAM HOME

Patty and Leroy worked together in their kitchen, baking a variety of casseroles with the sweet yams and green beans from their garden they'd canned a few months before. They were proud to share their season of hard work with the gathering at the Roberts' farm, and equally proud to be included.

Leroy pinched Patty on her plump rump as she bent over to open the oven door. Her giggle was infectious, and soon they both were laughing. Laughter had always been their strong point. It was part of what kept their thirty-some odd years together so very "together."

The only things they argued about were Patty's smoking and Leroy's nail biting. She hated with a passion how Leroy bit his nails down to the quick, and he hated her addiction to cigarettes. Neither issue was earth-shattering, but the two would repeat the same arguments a hundred times before they died, because they were the only things they disliked about each other.

Leroy was a widower when he met Patty. It happened in the parking lot of the post office one summer's day. She'd dropped her mail, scattering it all over the lot, just as Leroy pulled in after his first day of work as a mail carrier. Seeing her scrambling to retrieve her mail, he thought she was just the right size for a woman. Leroy liked meat on a woman's bones. Skinny women always reminded him of something out of National Geographic, a starving tribe member of one kind or another.

He parked his vehicle, then went over and bent down to help her pick up the envelopes, now blowing around the lot. But Leroy was doing more than grabbing mail off the ground; he was also peeking down Patty's shirt at her breasts. He hadn't meant to be rude, or seem like a pig, but those two large breasts dangled in front of him like a pair of playful devils, waving at him.

Suddenly, Leroy could feel her eyes boring into him. He'd been caught, and because he really wasn't a pig of a man, he was acutely embarrassed and felt the need to apologize; not for being a creep, but for being human. His tongue stuck in his throat when he raised his head to face her, because now he stared into the eyes of the most beautiful woman he'd ever seen. Those breasts were something, all right, but they were nothing compared to her face.

It was as if a spell had been cast in the post office parking lot that day. Two lonely people who thought that their destiny was to be single for the rest of their lives found each other.

Patty had never had a boyfriend. She always believed and accepted that no one would ever want her.

Self-conscious about her weight since child hood, due in part to her father's constant harsh remarks about her size. He called her 'chubby checkers' and 'fat ass', and not just in private either. He said that fat people were lazy, and for years she fantasized about standing up to him, especially about the lazy part, because it was her mother who supported the family, not him. Her dad sat on the couch all day watching TV in his underwear, while her mother worked like a dog at the bread factory in town, coming home to make dinner for him before even sitting down.

To say that his daughter resented him would be an understatement.

Patty wore her inferiority complex into adulthood, like a faded tattoo, and thanks to dear old dad it was always present, and grew uglier with age. She cried a lot back then, but not on the day her father died. Neither did her mother cry. Instead, they went to Red Lobster and celebrated their freedom.

"Hey honey", her husband asked as they worked on the casseroles. "How 'bout when we're done in here we treat ourselves and go to town for dinner? Maybe even have a drink or three, then when we come home we can play 'cops and robbers.' I'll be the cop and you be the robber."

Patty broke out in more laughter, but managed to squeak out, "Oh, I like being the bad one!"

CHARLES & ELIZA (SNOOPY PANTS) REEVE

Charles Reeve was busy unloading the wine from his truck to Eliza'a car. It was cheap carton wine, bought at Sam's Club, but they weren't connoisseurs, and they hoped the guests at the Roberts' farm weren't either. The Reeves weren't cheap. They were frugal, and proud of the way being careful with money had paid off in their lives.

Both of them had always worked, they just never made a lot of money doing it. It was only because they'd been 'bean counters' with the little money they made, that they had a home that was paid for, and were comfortable in their retirement.

They'd both grown up poor, and when you grow up that way you either learn how to be careful with money, or you spend it faster than you can make it. There's not a lot of in between. It's sort of like being an alcoholic. Either you swear off drinking, or you drink like a fish.

Not having grown up on farms, like many of their friends, meant that when the money ran out, so did the food. On a farm, when times were tough, the families might not have had much, but come meal time, there was always food on the table.

Being hungry as kids, was one of the few things Charles and Eliza had in common, and something neither of them would ever forget, nor wish on another living soul.

They'd pinched and saved for years so that their children could go to college. College wasn't an option in their household, but a requirement. They didn't want their children to struggle through life as they had. The Reeves believed that a college education was the ticket out of poverty, and they were right. Today, all three of their three children was a professional of one kind or another. That was the Reeves' single biggest accomplishment in life.

Charles still chose to work part-time by delivering pizzas on the weekends, but that wasn't because they needed the extra money as much as it was a chance for Charles to get out of the house and have space from his wife.

There was no question that they cared for one another, but they were as different as peas and carrots, compatible, but not alike. After fifty some odd years together, and with divorce not an option, they had learned how to make their marriage work and to appreciate each other. Having 'space,' as they call it today, worked for them.

While Charles was outside, Eliza sat in their living room with her feet up on a chair. Her ankles were swollen, a common occurrence nowadays. Not only was she short and overweight, but her volunteer schedule kept her on her feet far longer than any human being should be. But you couldn't tell her that. Eliza believed that the way to heaven was through good deeds, and if there truly was such a place as heaven, she most certainly deserved to be first in line. Her heart was as big as her ankles, if not bigger.

THE HAMILTONS

The Hamilton's were an ambitious young family, with jobs that sucked more than forty hours a week out of them. Tom was the head pharmacist at Walgreen's in Ottumwa, and Tennille was the manager of the largest grain mill in the county. Their ten-year-old twins, Jason and Kary Lynn, also had schedules nearly as time consuming as their parents.

By the time they all got home, there was often no time for home cooked meals, so Tennille would stop somewhere along her way and pick up a meal that someone else had made.

The American dream of his and her SUV's, sports, lavish vacations, and a house that was too big for one person to clean, cost their family a lot more than money.

With Thanksgiving a few hours away, Tennille felt stressed. The band was their contribution to the Roberts' festivities, and though that was welcomed by all who would attend, in itself it just wasn't enough for Tennille. She had been raised in a household where home-cooked meals were as natural as having two parents living together. It felt odd to not be making something yummy for Thanksgiving, because that wasn't the way she was raised. Cooking used to be the buildup to a holiday. It was what made a holiday feel like a holiday. She longed for the good old days, feeling guilty and disappointed in herself for allowing her busy life to get in the way of tradition.

Tennille stopped at the Canteen Lunch under the interstate bridge and purchased Maid Rites and fries on her way home. Inhaling the food as she drove the ten miles home, she promised herself that her priorities were going to change.

Tom was also on his way home, but first he had to pick up the kids from their swimming lessons at the Y. Usually, his drive home gave him time to unwind, but this evening was different. He felt unnerved as he thought about his wife and his kids. He suddenly realized that he missed them; missed them even though they were living under the same roof.

He knew he and his wife were growing apart, not because they were short on love, but because they were short on time. He decided that it was no longer acceptable.

His kids seemed unfazed by the lack of time they spent together, but out of all fairness how can someone miss something they haven't had? That question filled him with shame as he pulled into the lot at the Y and saw both of his children standing on the sidewalk, glued to their cell phones.

"Stuff!" He grumbled out loud. All of the stuff in the world simply couldn't replace what they were missing; each other. Tom sat in his car and watched his kids' little fingers move like lightning across the screens of their phones and he wondered just how long it would take for them to look up and see him sitting there. The shame he'd felt quickly morphed into annoyance. He honked the horn once, then kept his hand on it to embarrass them.

Embarrassment, if created without intent to harm, made a kid tough, he reasoned. He remembered back to when he was a teenager and 'too cool' to be seen with his parents, but his mother insisted that he go everywhere with them anyway. The minute his parents cleared the door of whatever store they dragged him into, he would go in the opposite direction, pretending to anyone who might give a damn that he was alone and definitely NOT with his parents.

Even though Tom couldn't have imagined it, his mother had once been a teenager herself, and she handled his embarrassment by embarrassing him even more. She would stand in the middle of an aisle and holler his name until she'd flushed him out of hiding, and he'd appear, just to shut her up. He was embarrassed alright, but her tactic toughened him up, enough that he eventually quit working so hard at being 'cool'.

His children both looked up in horror from their phones. Kary Lynn held up her arms and mouthed, "Enough, already!"

When they jumped in the car, and before they could tell him what a dork he was, he said, "Guess what we're not taking with us to Thanksgiving?"

MARY AND CHOD

Mary arrived home from school the evening before Thanksgiving and set about boiling water for the Jello desserts she was making for the feast. After filling the kettle, she sat down to pull off the shoes that were killing her feet, when she heard a knock at the door. She kicked her shoes to the side of the hallway where they hit the wall with a couple of loud thuds.

Opening the door, she was surprised to find Chod standing there.

"Hey, can I come in?" He asked through the screen door separating them.

She shrugged her shoulders, but quickly tried to pretend that she hadn't just done that, and opened the door wide enough for the huge man to pass through.

"Of course, is everything all right?"

The last time Mary had seen Chod was when he picked up her nephew at school to work at Fara's. She felt the same tug on her heart that day that she felt now.

"You wouldn't happen to have any coffee made, would you?" Chod asked, standing in the narrow hallway, way too close to her for comfort.

"I don't, but I can make some. Come on in and take a seat, it'll only take me a minute." The task of making coffee momentarily saved her. She damn near ran from the hallway and the unbearable closeness of this gentle giant.

Chod followed her into the kitchen and took a seat at the table. She could feel his eyes on her back.

Without turning around, she asked, "So what's up?"

When he didn't answer, she was forced to turn back around to face him again. He sat at her table with tears in his eyes, trying with everything he had to speak.

"Mary", he finally got out, "I know about your cancer. It's no secret, and of course I know about Leila having to go away again."

Clearing his throat, he looked straight at her. "I want you to know that I care. I have never stopped caring about you." He paused to wipe his eyes, then blow his nose with the handkerchief he'd pulled out of his back pocket.

Mary didn't know what to say, but she opened her mouth anyway, prepared to banish the awkwardness that hung in the air. But, before she could speak, he stood up and closed the distance between them.

She backed up as far as she could, until there was no more room to back up. She was against the counter, but he kept on coming. He was only inches away from her, forcing her to look up into his face or be smothered in the chest she'd so desperately missed.

"Mary, I came here today to tell you something and I'm not leaving until I do. I want to help you and I want you to let me help you."

Seeing the pain in her face, he continued, while he still had the stones.

"I love you, Mary, and even if you don't love me anymore, I want to help you. Please!" Then, just like that, he turned around and retreated to the chair at the table, as if what he'd just said took every ounce of energy he had and he had to sit down, or fall down.

She watched his large frame collapse into the chair. Mary felt like the wind had just been knocked out of her, but finally she opened her mouth again. This time words came out.

"Chod, you sweet man, I never stopped loving you. The only reason I stopped seeing you was because my life changed. I promised my sister I would take care of Dan, remember? I thought you understood that."

He nodded. "I did understand and I still do understand, but right now you don't have to take care of anybody but you, and I want to be with you as you go through this. The question is, will you let me?"

"What about Dan? And what about your work at the ranch?" She asked.

Now it was Mary closing the distance between them, standing right in front of the seated giant.

"My sister and brother will make sure Dan's okay, you know that", he said. "And the ranch won't miss me much. I figure I can spend the week with you in Des Moines and after your chemo treatments, we'll drive back home for the weekends. That way you can see Dan and I can catch up on my work."

The coffee maker hissed as it finished brewing, but they no longer cared about coffee.

Mary eased her way in between his legs, then with both hands cradled his balding head, she kissed the top of it before guiding it onto her chest.

"I was afraid you thought I had too many miles on me", he admitted, mumbling into her blouse.

"Never", she whispered.

The screen door opened, then slammed shut.

Chod's head snapped up and out of its cradle at lightning speed. But there was no time to stand up and pretend that there was a lot more than coffee brewing in that kitchen.

Mary froze, her face turning a color you wouldn't find on any color chart.

Leila walked into the kitchen and took in the scene at the table, a large grin spreading across her face. "Hi Chod", she said. "Long time-no see."

Before Chod could return the greeting, he heard Dan come barreling down the hallway, stopping in the kitchen doorway to see what everyone was up to.

He knew Chod was there, because he'd seen his truck parked out front.

Since, he just had the conversation with his mom about his living and working at the Kremer Ranch for a few months, he assumed Chod's visit was all business.

It took the poor kid a few minutes, before he caught onto the fact that his Aunt was holding his new employer's head in both hands, just a bit too close to her breasts.

When he did get the picture, everyone in the room watched as his mouth fell open, magnifying the empty whole where a tooth had once lived. The scene in the kitchen was quickly becoming comical. So much so that the adults in the room were working hard at suppressing their laughter.

Dan looked at his Aunt and then to Chod. Then he slowly shut his mouth and walked in closer, trying to assess exactly what was happening

"Chod?" He blurted out, "Are you all right, sir?"

Chod nodded, as a laugh escaped Leila's mouth.

Dan then looked at his Aunt; his blonde hair falling over his accusing

eyes and his mouth twisting in disgust. "Aunt Mary! What the heck are you doing to my boss?"

Mary could no longer contain herself. She cracked up.

Soon, everyone in the kitchen, including Dan, was laughing from somewhere deep down in their bellies, filling the small space with something long overdue, and as needed as marrow is to a bone.

PASTOR DALE & LINDA RAE

Pastor Dale had just finished his Wednesday confirmation class. The simple stone church was empty and quiet as he began stacking the chairs against the wall, while his wife, Linda, tidied up the room.

Both were eager to get home and start breading and frying a ridiculous amount of chicken livers, after which Linda was going to duplicate her grandmother's butter rolls for the feast.

It would be a late night in the kitchen, but an expected one this time of year.

Quietly, they anticipated the warmth and familiarity of the holidays as they tackled the tasks ahead.

Linda worked as fast as her diseased body would allow. Her MS was claiming more and more ownership of her limbs, leaving her with a numbness and an annoying fatigue, neither of which stopped her from being a part of whatever was going on.

Dale watched her work from across the room, remembering the day he'd first laid eyes on her. He thought at the time that she looked like the woman who played Wonder Woman in the TV series. In truth, she did, just without the outfit.

Watching her work now, with only one side of her body functioning, he decided she was indeed Wonder Woman. His wife never complained about what was happening to her mind and body. She believed her suffering was God's will. She trusted with all her heart and soul that she was chosen by Him to endure it, and for that reason alone she never complained.

Dale knew his wife was stronger than he was, when it came to self-lessness, admitting to her from time to time that he was angry with God, even as he watched her calmly accept transforming into a shadow of what she'd once been.

Linda knew each scripture upside and down, inside and out, and quoted appropriate ones whenever her husband needed to be pulled from the darkness of fear for her. She always had a way of making things make sense to him. It was a gift she had, one that had saved him so many years before.

In his late twenties, suffering from clinical depression, Dale lost his job and, with no family to turn to for help, he soon lost his apartment as well. Homeless and penniless, he ended up in a shelter, one where Linda was teaching bible studies twice a week.

He became interested in her teachings and after a few short months, he was committed to God. Three years later, he became pastor of his own church and husband to his very own 'Wonder Woman'.

Dale walked over to his wife as she wiped the last table and gently took her arm. "It's time we go home", he said. "You need to take a break before we dive into all that cooking. I'll run you a bath and while you're soaking I'll make us something good to eat. How's that sound, sweetie?"

Taking his offered arm, she said, "Sounds great, I'm pooped."

They were standing at the back door to the church, locking up, when the sound of footsteps came from behind them. Turning around, they found a wiry old man standing on the sidewalk, a duffel bag in one hand and a cigarette in the other. He was so thin that he looked like a strong wind could blow him down the street.

"Pastor Dale?" The man asked.

Dale nodded.

"I hear you're The Man", he said to Dale, then looked over at Linda and nodded again. "And I hear you're The Man too", he said with a toothless smile.

Automatically, moving between his wife and the stranger to protect her from potential danger, Dale asked, "What can we do for you, sir?"

"Name's Brian, Brian Archer", the stranger said. "I was told that you were the one to see if I needed help, and right now I'm in need of help."

With tenderness, Dale asked the man, "What kind of help are you looking for?"

"I'm waiting for a bed to open up at a treatment center in Des Moines. They say I can't get in until the Friday after Thanksgiving. I was hoping you could help me find a place to stay for the next two nights, and maybe lend me a couple bucks for something to eat."

"Archer?" Dale said. "I knew a guy named Archer once, a quarterback. I played football with him at ISU. You any relation?"

The man hung his head. "Once upon a time that was me, Dale. Don't blame you for not recognizing me. Once my dad died, I got caught up in some bad stuff. Spent all my money on drugs, even the money he left me. Lost my job, my wife and then my kids. Now here I am, alone and back in Ottumwa trying to pick up the pieces before there aren't any left to pick up."

The man's stained fingers released the cigarette, letting it fall to the ground, along with his duffel bag. Then he started to cry, like a baby into his dirty hands.

Dale walked away from his wife and over to the man he'd once known. He placed a hand on the bony shoulder and, with compassion, said, "You're not alone Brian. Jesus is your friend."

Brian removed his hands from his face.

"Dale, the only friend I've had up until recently goes by the name of 'Meth' and believe me, when I say that I'm ready for a different one."

"I believe you Brian," Dale said, walking back to the locked door.

He unlocked it, saying, "How about you and I a take a ride. I have a good friend who runs a shelter, called the Red Rooster Inn, out of an old farm in Eldon. He'll be happy to feed you and give you a bed for a couple of nights. Then when the treatment center's ready for you, I'll drive you there myself."

Before Brain could say anything, Linda added, "Brian, how about you go with Dale and get settled in, then we'll pick you up in the morning and you can spend Thanksgiving with us and some of our friends. There'll be plenty of food and, trust me, they won't mind."

"Sounds too good to be true", Brian twisted his upper lip into a smile and smoothed his shaggy hair over his forehead. Then in a poor attempt at an Elvis impersonation, he said, "Thank you. Thank you very much!" Bad as it was, it made Dale grin. He was more than happy to help Brian.

At the same time, he no longer really knew him, much less trusted him, so he turned around and walked his wife back into the church to wait for his return.

When they'd cleared the doors, she smiled and squeezed his hand. "This is going to be the best Thanksgiving ever."

"Dang tootin'," he agreed, with a wink.

BOY

Back at the Roberts' farm, Boy and his female double were playing in the fields, dodging both each other and the gentle snowflakes falling from the sky.

They played until they grew hungry and needed a break, which they took in the ancient oak tree on the levy near the river. After a few minutes of rest, Boy's friend took flight again, flitting from one rotten tree to another until finally settling on one near the fence line, she drilled relentlessly into its hollow core.

Her beak was stuffed with food ,when she landed back on the branch next to Boy. She leaned close to him, offering what she'd just worked so hard to gather, and he gobbled it right up.

As grateful as he was for the flies and abundance of sunflower seeds he'd been eating for the past few weeks, he had to admit that this meal was much more satisfying.

Pleased that he was pleased, she left the branch to go get more.

Boy felt embarrassed for not having the skills to find his own food. Apparently, hitting the window had cost him more than his ability to fly. Although his body was now strong, his memory was going to take a little more time to return.

Just as she arrived back at the tree with more food, a massive flock of birds flew over them in a synchronized pattern, then landed on the barren field just long enough to get the energy to do it again and again.

As they ate and watched the show, Boy could hardly believe his eyes. There were so many birds out there, and all of them looked like him.

His new lady love nestled in close, and when he turned to look into her big black eyes there was longing in them he couldn't ignore, lighting a flame in him that he never thought possible.

Finally, he knew what he must do.

He left the tree and flew across the field and pasture, passing the lounging Bob and Daisy, on his way to the house with the faded shutters.

He circled the chicken coop; the fearless Rooster being the only one outside, not bothered by the falling snow. Then, with no competition in sight, the large fowl pecked at the ground feverishly, looking up to acknowledge Boy as he passed over before returning to his feverish pecking.

Boy's heart pounded with excitement. "I am Boy", he sang at the top of his lungs.

Far off in the old oak tree came a faint return. "I know who you are Boy, and when you return to me I will teach you what you are."

Boy landed on the rotten window sill, inches from the window that had nearly cost him his life, and prepared to say goodbye. But when he looked through the glass his little heart sank.

Something was wrong. He could feel it. As he shook off the snow that was quickly coating his body he knew he couldn't leave, not now. And he knew the others wouldn't wait long for him. So be it, he told himself. If he was lucky, he would find them again in the spring.

A THANKSGIVING MIRACLE

Since Eileen's plans were to spend the entire day inside baking, she offered to watch Betty so that Old Man could be free to do as he pleased. She had no problem giving her mother-in-law a bath. She'd been giving her one on a regular basis for some time. Nor did she mind babysitting her, but this time Old Man had resisted.

He said he didn't want to go out today. The truth was that he didn't want to leave Wife's side.

"Something isn't right", he told Eileen.

"You don't spend most of your life with someone and not know these things", he added.

So, he sat on the couch next to Wife's chair all morning, making several unsuccessful attempts to read while she slept.

The only time he'd left the couch was to go to the bathroom, and let a meowing Mrs. Nickels out.

He caught Eileen peeking in at him a time or two from the kitchen where she was busy making and baking half a dozen pineapple upside-down cakes.

The house smelled like a home and he was grateful for that, more than he could ever say. If it were not for his concern for Wife, Eileen knew he'd be soaking up the feeling of Thanksgiving as she was.

She knew this because he was hungry for it, and it showed in everything he'd been doing up to this point.

But today, he was too preoccupied, watching his wife's chest rise and
fall, sitting on the edge of the couch ready to jump up at any moment.
Eileen worried because he worried.

"Something you want to talk about Hugh?" She asked from the kitch-
en, as she removed two golden pans from the oven and sat them on the
counter to cool.

She bent down and opened the oven door to put the last of the waiting
pans in, and hearing no answer from the other room, she walked towards
the counter that bordered the living room to see if Hugh and Betty were
still there.

They were, but Hugh was no longer on the edge of the couch. He was
on the floor, kneeling in front of the chair that held a limp body. Betty's
head hung to one side like a rag doll. Her small mouth was open enough
to see her tongue, hanging half in and half out. Old Man's head lay in
her lap, his large body convulsing silently with pain.

"Oh my God", Eileen cried, taking it all in and running to them. She
got down on the floor behind Hugh and put her arms as far around him
as she could.

Her left hand reached up for the tiny wrist that dangled over the arm of
the chair. There was no pulse. Betty was gone, but this time she wouldn't
be found in the yard or the chicken coop. She was 'gone', gone.

"I'm so sorry, Hugh. So, so sorry", she whispered into the back of his
flannel shirt.

They stayed that way for a few minutes before he lifted his head. "Did
you know that, in her day, Betty was a hell of a dancer?" Eileen shook
her head, even though she did know. She let him ramble. "She was one
hell of dancer, best dance partner I ever had. I guess she was the only
dance partner I ever had", he mumbled, a small laugh escaping, as the
tears ran down his face.

"I know it sounds selfish, but I was really looking forward to Thanksgiving, so we could dance again. Just one more dance. Damn it!"

Then he lay his head back down and sobbed some more.

It wasn't selfish at all, and as much as Eileen wanted to tell him that,
she kept quiet. This was his time. Even so, she wasn't going to leave him
alone. Not now, not ever.

Eileen rested her head back down on his large back and listened to his
sobs, feeling more helpless than she'd felt in her entire life.

After a while, she felt a tug on her hair. It was snagged or caught
somewhere on Old Man's shirt. She lifted her head after feeling a par-

ticularly hard pull on her hair, and when she looked up, what she saw actually knocked her over.

"Holy shit!" She gasped, falling backwards onto the floor, and startling Old Man. He lifted his head and looked back at her, but all she could do was point.

Old Man's eyes followed her pointing finger back to the chair. He too gasped when he saw a wide-eyed Wife starring back, holding a tuft of Eileen's hair in her hand.

Old Man jumped up off the floor and bent over to hold his wife, his no longer "dead" wife.

However, Wife would have none of it. She slapped her stunned husband away like a bothersome fly.

"She's back!" He said, breathlessly straightening his old body. "By God, she's back!"

Eileen, who was in some serious shock at the moment, stayed put on the floor. She'd heard of people waking up from a coma, but not death. Never ever had she heard of anyone coming back from the dead, not in real life anyway. Could this be real?

The utter quiet in that room was so profound that you could hear the old house creak. At last, Old Man offered his hand to Eileen and helped her to her feet. They stood facing each other, both still in total disbelief, when the timer on the stove sounded, breaking the spell.

Before reaching the kitchen counter, Eileen turned back to look at Old Man and the now animated Wife, just to make sure that what just happened had happened.

With a new urgency, she removed the cakes from the oven, then hurried back to the living room, where Old Man once again sat on the couch. She saw that his hands formed a steeple, and his eyes looked up to the stained ceiling above, and his lips moved, but no sound came out.

Wife sat unaware in her chair by the window, just as she usually did, contentedly watching the snow fall outside.

When Eileen's gaze moved from Old Man to Wife, she saw Wife smile at her own reflection in the glass. And looking towards the window too, Eileen caught the briefest glimpse of something else, the back of a bird as it lifted into the snowy night and flew away.

Eileen's eyes darted back and forth from Old Man to Wife.

"Hugh, don't you think we should take Betty to the hospital, just to get her checked out?" She thought that possibly she might need to be checked out too.

"No honey, I don't", he replied. "Whatever is going to happen to this woman is going to happen to her right here, in her own house and on her own farm." Old Man glanced over to Wife, then added, smiling, "Besides, I believe the Lord has already checked her out."

Eileen didn't know what to say, so she walked over to him and placed a hand on his face, where his tears had already dried. She was so thankful that Jacob was at school. Nothing she had seen just now could be explained, not in a million years. She thought that whoever said that a parent has the answer to everything was just, well, full of shit.

Like a robot, she turned around, walked into the kitchen, and opened the cabinet door above the sink, the one that held the brandy. Then she poured herself a shot and, as she raised the glass to her lips, she glanced again out the window in time to see a swarm of birds flying by. As if on cue, they reversed direction, landing on the ground just outside.

Numb with shock and wonder, Eileen watched a single bird leave the group and fly over to the window, hovering in the air right in front of her. The tiny bird was so close, that if the window pane hadn't separated them, she could have reached out and touched its wings.

Bird and woman locked eyes, then it jetted away, returning to others, who seemed to be waiting for it to return. Then they disappeared, as if they'd never been there at all.

With a shaky hand, Eileen opened the cabinet door and again took down the bottle of brandy, this time filling the glass to the brim. Warm tears ran down her cheeks as she downed the liquor like the pro she wasn't.

Once the choking and gagging subsided, Eileen caught her breath and leaned against the sink, thinking about how there was no way in hell she would ever forget what just happened. With hesitation, she raised her head to look out the window, uncertain of what might await her on the other side.

Her heart smiled when all she saw was Jacob, skipping up the gravel driveway towards the house, wearing a paper hat shaped like a turkey. And her thoughts turned to the big day ahead and of her gratitude for the gift of life, and even death. The good, the bad and the ugly, the numb nuts and the dick weeds; she was thankful for all of it.

And she whispered, to no one in particular, or possibly to everyone and everything, "Thanksgiving, here we come!"

.

THE END

Made in the USA
Coppell, TX
12 June 2020

27486450R00075